Three women

Years ago Gemma, Zoe and Violet all took the same college sex-ed class, one they laughingly referred to as Sex for Beginners. It was an easy credit—not something they'd ever need in real life. Or so they thought...

Their professor had them each write a letter, outlining their most private, most outrageous sexual fantasies. They never dreamed their letters would be returned to them when they least expected it. Or that their own words would change their lives forever...

Don't miss Stephanie Bond's newest miniseries:

Sex for Beginners

WATCH AND LEARN
(October 2008)

IN A BIND
(November 2008)

NO PEEKING...
(December 2008)

Sex for Beginners
What you don't know...might turn you on!

Blaze™

Dear Reader,

Have you ever run across an old childhood diary or a note you wrote in high school or college? It can be fun, and even revealing, to see what you were thinking when you were younger, what things were important to you.

The seniors at Women's Covington College who took the Sexual Psyche class (dubbed by the students as "Sex for Beginners") were given an assignment to write down their innermost sexual fantasies in the form of a letter to themselves. Their letter was to be cataloged with a code for anonymity and remain sealed for ten years, then mailed to them.

When international flight attendant Zoe Smythe reads her letter, she's headed to Sydney, Australia, for a leisurely layover before returning to America to be married. The naughty words she wrote years ago spur her to embark on a last-chance torrid fling with a hunky Aussie.... But will she ever want to leave?

I hope you enjoy *In a Bind*, the second book in the SEX FOR BEGINNERS trilogy. Please tell your friends about the wonderful stories you find between the pages of Harlequin novels! And visit me at www.stephaniebond.com.

Happy endings always,

Stephanie Bond

STEPHANIE BOND
In a Bind

TORONTO • NEW YORK • LONDON
AMSTERDAM • PARIS • SYDNEY • HAMBURG
STOCKHOLM • ATHENS • TOKYO • MILAN • MADRID
PRAGUE • WARSAW • BUDAPEST • AUCKLAND

ISBN-13: 978-0-373-79438-6
ISBN-10:   0-373-79438-X

IN A BIND

This edition published by arrangement with Harlequin Books S.A.

® and TM are trademarks of the publisher. Trademarks indicated with ® are registered in the United States Patent and Trademark Office, the Canadian Trade Marks Office and in other countries.

www.eHarlequin.com

Printed in U.S.A.

ABOUT THE AUTHOR

Stephanie Bond credits romance novels with teaching her world history and geography and for giving her a case of wanderlust. It seemed only natural that she would someday be writing romance novels herself. To date, Stephanie has written more than forty romance and mystery novels, and doesn't plan on slowing down anytime soon at what she considers to be "her dream job." Stephanie lives in midtown Atlanta with her hunky architect/artist/hero husband.

Books by Stephanie Bond

Don't miss any of our special offers. Write to us at the following address for information on our newest releases.

Harlequin Reader Service
U.S.: 3010 Walden Ave., P.O. Box 1325, Buffalo, NY 14269
Canadian: P.O. Box 609, Fort Erie, Ont. L2A 5X3

For Brenda, of course,
for throwing aside the reins

1

"JUST THINK—THIS IS YOUR LAST trip as an unmarried woman."

Zoe Smythe kept nodding and welcoming aboard first-class passengers on the Atlanta flight bound for Sydney, Australia, trying to ignore her friend Erica's comment. "Welcome aboard.... Good evening.... May I take your coat?"

Erica leaned in. "Are you going to do something wild and outrageous during your layover in Sydney after I leave?"

Zoe gave a dry laugh. "Hardly. I brought a stack of things that have to be finalized for the wedding."

"That doesn't sound like fun," Erica said, then elbowed Zoe. "Welcome to married life." Erica cackled at her own joke. "Well, for the two days that I'm there, I propose that we ingest large amounts of alcohol and take up residence in the hotel spa."

"Sounds good," Zoe agreed.

"Maybe we'll get lucky and our masseuse will be a big, strapping Aussie."

"Maybe." Zoe bit back a smile. Erica's marriage was sex-starved.

"Seriously, though, I'm going to miss having you on this route, Zoe."

"Thanks, but a domestic route will allow me to be home more."

"You'll be changing back after a couple of years," Erica said drily.

Zoe frowned good-naturedly, then turned her attention back to the passengers.

"Welcome aboard…. Good evening…. May I take your coat?"

"Yes, thank you."

At the sound of the thick Australian accent, Zoe tipped up her head to meet the gaze of the clearest, greenest eyes she'd ever seen, slightly hooded and set off with straight, sun-tipped lashes. The man behind them was tall with coarse blond hair cut close to his head and a five o'clock shadow on his square jaw. Zoe sucked in a breath. The stranger exuded raw masculinity. The leather duster he shrugged out of was the color of baked ocher, conjuring up images of the parched land of the Outback. Beneath the rugged coat he wore an impeccably cut gray business suit, although his shirt collar was open and his tie loosened.

A corporate cowboy? How…intriguing. "Did you enjoy your stay in Atlanta, sir?" she asked as she took his coat and suit jacket.

"I did," he said with a smile. "But it's always nice to get back home and sleep in my own bed."

It was an innocent enough statement, one she'd heard travelers say countless times during her stint as a flight attendant. But something about the way he said it conjured up images of the big man sprawled naked in a giant bed made of hand-hewn logs. Zoe gave herself a mental shake. What was wrong with her?

"If I may see your boarding pass, sir, I'll show you to your seat."

He handed her the document and her pulse spiked—he was sitting in her section. She glanced at his name—Colin Cannon—then handed back his boarding pass. "Mr. Cannon, right this way."

Zoe felt his gaze on her back as he followed her, and was absurdly glad she'd taken pains with her appearance. She'd worn one of the sharper uniforms in her work wardrobe, a black skirt and a thin dove-gray wrap sweater, and had twisted her dark brown hair into a low knot on the nape of her neck. She chastised herself for caring what she looked like for this passenger—it wasn't the behavior of a woman who was a month away from marrying the man of her dreams.

"Here you are, sir, seat 4A. My name is Zoe and I'll be seeing to your needs during the first half of the flight." Standing so close, she had to look straight up at the tall man. The proximity unnerved her and suddenly her small talk seemed laced with innuendo.

"Zoe—pretty name." He was unbuttoning his shirtsleeves, rolling them up, revealing powerful arms that were tanned and covered with light-colored hair.

"Th-thank you. Would you like a cocktail before we take off?"

"A vodka on the rocks would be great, thanks."

Zoe was relieved to step into the tiny galley to prepare the drink. To her dismay, her heart thudded against her breastbone and her face felt warm.

"Lucky dog," Erica whispered in her ear. "You always get the hunks."

"Trade me sections," Zoe said earnestly.

Erica squinted. "Why?"

Zoe's mind raced for an excuse. "Uh…I'm getting a vibe from Mr. 4A."

Erica leaned backward to glance at the topic of conversation.

Zoe grabbed her friend's arm. "Don't look! He'll know we're talking about him."

Erica grinned. "So? What kind of vibe are you talking about? He certainly doesn't look like a perv."

"No, he's not a perv. He's…um…"

"He's *hot*." Then Erica gasped. "Oh my goodness—you *like* him, don't you?"

Zoe scoffed. "That's crazy. I'm getting married in a month, remember?" Feeling out of sorts, she touched Erica's arm. "Look, just do me this favor, okay?"

Erica shrugged. "Fine with me. But I warn you, the couple in 8A and B seem to be on the verge of a divorce."

Zoe picked up the drink she'd poured. "Thanks. I'll deliver this, then check in with your warring couple."

Exhaling in relief, she walked back to Colin

Cannon's seat where his big body took up every inch of the generous space, his long legs extending to the bulkhead in front of him. The man was vast and unrestrained, like his mother country.

As he lifted his head, he raked his gaze over her legs and every inch of her until he made eye contact. At his appreciative stare, a vacuum seemed to develop around them—her ears popped as if the cabin was changing pressure. There was something about this man that spoke to her...confused her. With a mere glance, he made everything female deep inside her open and expand. Her breathing increased, her throat tightened. Swapping sections with Erica was definitely the right move, she decided. There was something...*unmanageable* here that she dared not explore.

Her hand shook slightly as she gave him the drink—with good reason. When his fingers brushed hers, a current of awareness shot up her arm. Strangely, a sense of déjà vu tickled her memory, but she couldn't put her finger on why. Nor did she want to.

"Mr. Cannon," she said, "as it turns out, I won't be taking care of this section after all."

Disappointment flashed across his face. "Did I scare you off?"

Zoe swallowed. "It has nothing to do with you, sir."

He looked as if he didn't believe her, then lifted his glass. "Cheers, then."

She nodded and walked away, troubled by the regret that plucked at her...as if she had turned her back on a life-changing encounter. Something wonderful…or something dangerous. When she stole a glance over her shoulder at the golden-haired Aussie, he was still looking at her with those intense green eyes.

Zoe turned back and manufactured a smile for the young professional couple that Erica had warned her about. Indeed, Jill and Jeremy Osbourne were shooting daggers at each other and trading barbs in tones that did not bode well for the long trip ahead of them. Worse, they seemed determined to draw Zoe into their squabble.

"What do you think about a woman who packs twenty-three pairs of designer shoes for a ten-day trip?" Jeremy Osbourne asked, his words wrapped in sarcasm.

"What do you think about a man who brings his laptop on his second honeymoon?" Jill Osbourne asked in a matching tone.

"Is this your first trip to Australia?" Zoe asked cheerfully.

"Yes," they said in unison, both sounding miserable.

"I wanted to go to Hawaii," the woman said, her voice accusing.

"I thought this would be an adventure," her husband retorted.

"And you expect me to believe that this trip has nothing to do with the fact that your biggest client is in Sydney?" his wife shrieked.

"My job pays for your shoes!" he returned.

"Sydney is a romantic choice for your second honeymoon," Zoe soothed.

"Are you married?" Jill Osbourne asked.

"In one month," Zoe said with a smile.

"You still have time to reconsider," the woman said pointedly.

"It's certainly not all it's cracked up to be," her husband agreed with a shake of his newspaper.

The tension between the couple was palpable. They knew every button to push and continued to antagonize each other over a sumptuous meal of surf and turf. The rich red wine only seemed to fuel their long-running argument. Zoe bit her tongue and wondered why they bothered staying married if they provoked each other so bitterly. If she and Kevin ever argued like that…

She shook her head. She and Kevin would never end up like that. Would they?

They had been together for nearly six years, engaged for half that time. They knew each other so well, sometimes she felt as if they already were married. It was comforting to be so…comfortable. She couldn't imagine her and Kevin being at each other's throats the way this couple was. They infected everybody around them.…

Instilled doubts.

Which was silly, because no marriage was perfect, was it? She had a healthy grasp of Kevin's idiosyncrasies, and vice versa. It was good, wasn't it, that they were friends first, lovers second? And it was good that they didn't agree on everything—it meant that they both had to compromise. Not that they would end up like this feuding couple…or her own quarrelsome parents…or Kevin's.

Her anxiety level was driven higher by the fact that she felt the Aussie's gaze on her as she moved about the first-class cabin, especially when they stopped in San Francisco to refuel and most passengers took advantage of the opportunity to stretch their legs. He paced the aisle, his big body taking up much of the available space. Even first class wasn't designed for men of his size. She wondered vaguely if he was a professional athlete. Colin Cannon had descended from a pretty spectacular gene pool, and despite the immaculate suit, his body wasn't that of a man who sat behind a desk for most of his day.

Their eyes met and a shiver of feminine appreciation traveled up her spine. She was as aware of him as if they were sitting next to each other, knees touching. It was strange, feeling as though everyone else on the plane were extras in a private little drama between the two of them. How could she feel such a powerful connection to a person with whom she'd exchanged only a few words?

She couldn't, she decided, dragging her gaze from his. It was an illusion brought on by the thin air, fatigue and nerves over the unfinished wedding details that still needed to be handled. She tried to put the man out of her mind as the final and longest leg of their flight got under way, tending to the pas-

sengers in her section, including the high-mainte-
nance, sniping couple.

By the time her shift had ended somewhere over
the Pacific Ocean, the Osbournes had, mercifully,
fallen asleep along with most of the other passengers.
The cabin was dark except for the lone reading light
illuminating the man in 4A. He appeared to be
immersed in some sort of thick, bound report, his
head bent in thought, his hands moving occasionally
to mark a page.

She wanted to ask him what business he was in
or if he needed a blanket, anything to hear the
pleasing inflection of his accent. Her body tingled,
strained toward him, even with multiple rows of seats
dividing them. It was an alien feeling. She never
flirted with passengers or took advantage of the
many opportunities to hook up with single *and*
married men during her travels. She had always been
faithful to Kevin, had never even considered getting
herself into a situation that could get out of hand.

Until now. There was something so compelling
about this man. Zoe half wished she hadn't traded
sections with Erica. Perhaps during the flight she
would've learned something about him that would've
rendered him less appealing. He could be married…with a house full of kids…involved in shady
business dealings…a male chauvinist…with objec-
tionable views on the human condition.

As if he sensed her attention, he turned his head
and smiled, then gestured her over.

Zoe had no choice but to comply. Her heart rate increased with every step. She stopped next to his seat and leaned close so their conversation wouldn't wake the other passengers. "Yes, Mr. Cannon?"

"I'm sorry to bother you, Zoe, but I left something in the pocket of my suit jacket and I didn't see where you hung it."

He smelled of some lingering, unidentifiable spice that warmed her lungs. "I'll get it for you," she murmured.

"Thank you." His mouth curved into a smile that extended to his remarkable, sexy eyes that simmered with just enough merriment to dispel any idea she might have had that he was dangerous.

The coat closet took her out of his range of sight, which gave her a few minutes to compose herself. She was behaving like a schoolgirl, allowing a man's physical presence to affect her. This wasn't like her. She put her hand to her forehead and acknowledged the elevated heat. Maybe she was coming down with something. She exhaled slowly. Yes, with a little rest and a couple of aspirin, she'd be back to herself again.

Zoe found Mr. Cannon's jacket and pulled it out of the closet. When she folded it over her arm, though, something fell out of the inside breast pocket and landed by her foot. A black jeweler's box—ring size. She scooped it up and looked all around to make sure she was alone. Stroking the velvety surface, she fought the urge to peek inside. An engagement ring, perhaps? It seemed likely, since Mr. Cannon wasn't wearing a wedding ring.

It was the crazy, unreasonable pang of jealousy toward the unknown woman that brought her back to earth. This was insane—she should be thinking about the engagement ring on her *own* finger rather than worrying about the possible romantic liaisons of a perfect stranger.

Disgusted with herself, she dropped the box back into the coat pocket and carried it to him. He nodded his thanks and reached into a different pocket to remove a PDA device. "I hate this thing," he said ruefully, "but I can't live without it."

Apparently his mind hadn't been on whatever was in the box—just like hers shouldn't be.

"Mr. Cannon, the crew is getting ready to change, so if there's nothing else, I'll say goodbye."

Interest lit his eyes. "You're going off duty?"

Dismayed by the way her body responded to his slightest signal, she moistened her lips. "Yes. Enjoy the remainder of the flight."

She straightened and moved down the aisle to confer with the attendant who would be taking over her section. Erica walked up, wearing a frown. "Gee, that hunky Aussie is a dreamboat, Zoe, but he's kind of boring. Although he did seem to watch you pretty closely…."

"I didn't notice," Zoe said lightly.

Erica looked intrigued. "If you say so. How was the married couple?"

"Still married, miraculously." Zoe retrieved her shoulder bag from storage. It was silly, but she was the tiniest bit glad to know that Colin Cannon hadn't hit on the vivacious, blond Erica—he wasn't a player after all.

Not that it mattered to her.

A few minutes later, she sank into the assigned coach seat she would occupy for the six hours remaining in the flight.

She should've gone to sleep immediately. Her body was tired and her lower back ached. But her mind refused to shut down, not ready to turn away from the Aussie in first class whose green eyes had scoured her body with unabashed sexual interest. It was flattering…made her feel vibrant and desirable. Because as much as she was sure of Kevin's love for her, he wasn't exactly the passionate type. Sex ranked somewhere below fantasy football and training for his next long-distance bike race. They hadn't slept together in weeks because of their schedules and all the wedding preparations. She'd convinced herself it was okay—it would make the honeymoon even sweeter.

But she was lonely…and Kevin's inattentiveness had left her feeling as if she'd sprung a leak.

Before her mind spun off in a dangerous direction, she pulled out the three-ring binder that contained all the details of "Zoe and Kevin's Wedding." Inside were pages and pages of samples and order forms and receipts and schedules. Still to be decided was the seating arrangement at the rehearsal dinner and the reception, the music mix for the band, the decorations for the head tables, gifts for the wedding party and the marriage license.

As well as roughly one thousand other details.

From her bag she pulled her mail that she'd bound with a rubber band. Lately her box was crammed with brochures from photographers, caterers, florists and travel agencies. But scattered among the advertisements were contracts that needed to be reviewed and signed, and invoices that needed to be paid. She flipped through the envelopes and fished out a bill from the bridal shop, a reservation form for the limo service and a contract from the videographer. There were cards from friends and relatives who couldn't make it to the wedding—she and Kevin would open those later.

She glanced at the next envelope, which had a return address of Jacksonville, Florida—something from Covington Women's College? Then she smiled. It was probably a copy of the alumni newsletter, featuring a notice of her upcoming wedding. Grateful for a little light reading, she opened the envelope. But instead of a newsletter, she pulled out a cover letter enclosing a purple envelope that seemed distantly familiar. Intrigued, she scanned the letterhead—*Dr. Michelle Alexander*.

Zoe frowned. Her former college instructor?

Dear Ms. Smythe,

You were a student in my senior-level class titled "Sexual Psyche" at Covington Women's College. You may or may not recall that one of the optional assignments in the class was for each student to record her sexual fantasies and seal them in an envelope, to be mailed to the student in ten years' time. Enclosed you will find the envelope that you submitted, which was carefully cataloged by a numbered code for the sake of anonymity and remained sealed. It is my hope that the contents will prove to be emotionally constructive in whatever place and situation you find yourself ten years later. If you have any questions, concerns or feedback, do not hesitate to contact me.

With warm regards,

Dr. Michelle Alexander

Zoe laughed to herself. The Sexual Psyche class had been called Sex for Beginners by all the students. She remembered the class, the smothered giggles and eye-opening lectures, the confident, curvy instructor. She also remembered the confess-your-fantasies assignment, but she couldn't recall what she'd written.

Fingering the purple envelope, Zoe was suddenly nervous. She was on the verge of getting married. Was this really the best time in her life to review what sexual desires had once stirred her soul?

2

ZOE STARED AT THE ENVELOPE holding the letter she'd written to herself ten years ago and scoffed at her fears. What was she afraid of? The purple envelope wasn't exactly Pandora's box—it wasn't likely to unleash some sort of unforeseeable chain of events. Instead, she'd probably get a good laugh over her schoolgirl musings.

She glanced at the passengers sitting on either side of her—the woman to her left was awake, but reading a book. The woman to her right was juggling a sleeping toddler. With her privacy assured, Zoe slipped her finger under the flap of the envelope and pulled out two folded sheets of stationery. The handwriting was hers, neat and slanted. Pulled along by nostalgia, Zoe read the letter she'd written for her eyes only.

Dear Zoe,
It's me—your twenty-two-year-old self writing to say that when you get this letter, I hope you have everything in our life figured out. I hope you're married to a great guy and contemplat-

ing a family. I say this because I hope between now and then, you will have explored the world and yourself, and will be satisfied that your choices are good ones.

Dr. Alexander asked us to write down our sexual fantasies because she says that unless we know what turns us on physically, we can't ask for it or expect it from our partners. And that we'll never be truly fulfilled in a long-term relationship unless our partner knows and understands our innermost fantasies, no matter how outrageous they might be. She says that the strongest emotional connection comes from an intense physical connection, and a strong physical connection is the foundation for intimacy and fidelity. If someone is getting everything they need from one person, Dr. Alexander says, they'll have no need to stray.

I like the sound of that because fidelity is very important to me. On the other hand, I wouldn't want someone to be with me and not be completely happy…like my parents. Arguing is their only form of communication. I want to ask them sometimes why they stay together because they obviously don't like each other. I hope they're not together for my sake because they're miserable, and I'm miserable when they fight.

Anyway, I haven't had that much experience with sex. I'm not a virgin, but so far, to be honest, sex has been disappointing. Every time I've gone all the way with a guy, I hoped it was going to be the way I imagined sex would be—mind-blowing. Like a drug, something you can't live without. But it never is.

Maybe it's my fault. Because I'm outgoing and I speak my mind, I think guys assume that I want to take control. I've never told anyone that what I really want is to *give up* control. What I really want in my secret of secret places is to be tied to a bed…to be handcuffed…to be strapped down. And to be made love to six different ways.

Zoe looked up from the letter, her face heated. The words made her squirm in her seat—it must have taken a great effort for her to write them ten years ago. And if she remembered correctly, a great relief. With no small amount of trepidation, she continued reading.

It sounds dirty, which is why I've kept this to myself. I'm not looking for someone to mistreat me—I don't want that kind of man in my life. But someday I hope I'll meet the right guy to share my fantasy, someone I trust not to hurt me, someone who won't judge me, who won't think any less of me for wanting to explore the darker side of sex, the pleasure and the pain. Someone who knows when to stop, and when to push beyond. Someone who is also looking for that deep emotional and physical bond that Dr. Alexander described to us.

So, Zoe, wherever you are, I hope you found that guy. For both our sakes.

Zoe glanced up from the letter, her heart thudding. Her mind sifted through the internal revelations unveiled in what was supposed to be an innocent letter written by a naive college student. Instead it planted seeds of troubling thoughts. What if the naive letter writer had had more insight and wisdom than her grown-up self? She put her hand over her mouth, shaken by the prophetic words she'd written as a young woman.

"Are you okay?" the woman next to her asked kindly.

Zoe turned her head and registered that the woman was beautiful—short, spiky black hair with a pink streak and oddly colored eyes. Maybe violet? It was hard to tell in the low lighting. "I'm fine, thank you."

"I hope that isn't bad news," the woman said, nodding to the letter.

Zoe hastily refolded the letter and tucked it back into the envelope. "No. Just a note from an old friend, that's all."

"Oh, that's nice. Is it someone you miss?"

Zoe considered the question and her mind went back to the person she'd been in college...full of optimism and adventure, determined to meet the world and people in it on her own terms, determined not to settle for less than supreme happiness and a one-of-a-kind love.

"Yes, I do miss her," she said wistfully.

"Then maybe you should plan a little reunion." The woman winked and turned back to her book.

It was an interesting suggestion, Zoe conceded— getting in touch with the woman she'd been ten years ago. Curious, carefree and thrill-seeking. Traveling all over the world, fearlessly sampling different cultures. Then one day she'd looked around and all of her girl-friends had paired off with men they planned to marry. Zoe's mother began to pressure her to settle down. Someone introduced her to Kevin, and they'd hit it off.

And somewhere along the way, she'd become a paler version of herself, like a favorite shirt that had been laundered too many times, but was still ser-viceable enough to wear to the grocery store.

Yet before she gave in to the panic tickling her stomach, Zoe stopped. Did she still feel the same way about sex and love? Did she still entertain the same fantasies?

Yes, she realized with a sinking heart. When Kevin made love to her, she closed her eyes and imagined all the things he *wasn't* doing to her.

So had she made a good choice? Had she found the right man to marry?

She visualized telling Kevin that she wanted him to tie her to the bed or to lash her down with his leather belt. He would laugh at her. Kevin was a congenial fellow whose mind didn't go to dark places, especially where sex was concerned. He'd been scandalized when she'd once suggested they rent an X-rated movie on pay-per-view. He was a meat-and-potatoes missionary man. And since all of his intimate parts had fit hers generally well, she'd decided that bondage fantasies were for women who wanted to remain single. Forgoing her darkest desires seemed a small price to pay for dependability and friendship.

Her hand tightened around the letter. Dependability? Friendship? It sounded as if she was talking about a dog, not the man she was going to spend the rest of her life with. Kevin would be her last bed partner. Was theirs a one-of-a-kind love, or were they simply good together? Were both of them simply relieved that they didn't argue like both sets of their parents? What they had was fine...

But was it enough to bind herself to him for the rest of her life?

And why was her mind suddenly filled with the image of a pair of hooded green eyes?

COLIN REACHED THE LAST PAGE of the annual report, then realized he couldn't remember a word of what he'd just read. He pulled a hand down his face and reread two paragraphs before giving up and closing the report.

That woman—Zoe. Did she realize that she'd hit him like a ton of bricks?

Colin laughed to himself. His mother's Americanisms had rubbed off on him. Virginia Cannon teased him no end when one of her phrases slipped out of his mouth. And she would be intrigued to know that an American woman had captured his attention—a *Southern* American woman, no less. Like his mother.

Maybe it was Zoe's rich Southern accent that captivated him, because it reminded him of his mother's lilting, loving voice. But he'd met countless southern women on his many trips to Atlanta and none of them had affected him this way. He prided himself on being in control of his body and his mind. So when a woman hijacked his focus with a prim uniform and a handful of conversation, it was unsettling. Especially since she, too, seemed to be resisting the unexpected attraction between them.

Colin turned in his seat, but the first-class cabin was still dark and he couldn't see past the curtain leading to coach. She was back there somewhere, wedged into a small seat among grumpy salespeople and crying babies. Had she felt the electricity between them? Was she thinking about him, too? Wondering what might've happened if they'd met under different circumstances…what could still happen?

He'd never joined the mile-high club; in fact, he'd never even considered it. And he was pretty damned sure that a flight attendant could get fired for doing something as illicit as having sex in the loo. But he knew he couldn't go another minute without finding out if she was as curious about this *thing* between them as he was.

Colin pushed to his feet, then turned and strode down the aisle, headed for the coach cabin. He could live with rejection—but not regret.

He wasn't sure he'd be able to find her in the semidark cabin and he had no idea what he was going to say. How did one proposition someone on an airplane? Blood rushed through his ears as he scanned the rows of passengers. His pulse jumped higher when he saw her, chewing on her thumbnail, seemingly lost in thought. He stopped, noting with frustration that she was sitting in the center of several packed rows. It would be hard to get her attention without disturbing others, without making a fool out of himself.

He stopped and reconsidered. This was madness, after all, feeling so physically drawn to this woman that he was pursuing her at ten thousand meters in the air.

But then Zoe looked up and saw him, sending lust ripping through his body like an arrow. Her expression went from surprised to questioning.

He straightened and jammed his hands on his hips. At a loss, he tried to communicate to her what he was thinking by holding her gaze. Her mouth parted, her eyes softened. When after almost a minute she didn't look away, he took a deep breath, then nodded as imperceptibly as possible toward the bay of loos in the center of the plane. She understood because she pressed her lips together.

Colin turned and made his way to one of the cubicles, acknowledging wryly that his cock was as stiff as a lad's. He sincerely hoped that the lovely Zoe decided to join him. One way or another he would have to find release, and he'd much prefer to do it with her than without her.

ZOE SAT STOCK-STILL, afraid to move. In the midst of her musings, Colin Cannon had appeared like a mirage and made it clear that he'd come looking for her. And now he was waiting for her to join him in the lavatory. Had she been sending him vibes? How else could he have known that she was sitting in the back thinking about him?

Because he'd been sitting in the front thinking about *her*.

On some level she wasn't entirely surprised. From the moment he'd boarded the plane, something unexplainable had sprung up between them. Their mouths said polite things to each other, but their bodies had been having an entirely different conversation.

And now the moment of truth. Did she dare go to him? She twisted the engagement ring on her hand, trying to plant the image of Kevin in her mind. Fidelity was still very important to her.

On the other hand, they weren't married yet…. She hadn't taken any vows. Kevin never had to know. She could sample this bizarre, compulsive lust that she felt for the Aussie, and it would all be over by the time they landed.

Zoe glanced around to see if anyone else had noticed him singling her out. The black-haired woman next to her was absorbed in her book. Erica sat in the row behind her, fast asleep. The cabin was still dark, but everyone would be rousing soon as they flew into daylight. It was now or never.

As if she were watching someone else, Zoe picked up her flight bag that contained a change of clothes and headed toward the row of lavatories. Her limbs were almost weak with apprehension—or was it anticipation? She might regret this terribly.

Yet somehow, she didn't think so.

3

ZOE STARED AT THE ROW of four lavatory doors, her heart in her throat. Which one was he in?

Two of them read *Vacant,* so she knocked lightly and tried those first, but they were both empty. She approached the first door that read *Occupied,* and after a bolstering breath, rapped lightly. The sign clicked to *Vacant,* meaning the door had been unlocked. Zoe swallowed hard and glanced all around to make sure no one saw her going inside. And she told herself that she could still change her mind.

But even through the door she could feel his pull on her and was almost powerless to resist him. She had to find out why this man could entice her into doing things that she wouldn't have considered mere hours ago.

She twisted the handle, pushed open the door and slipped inside.

The space was generous by airplane facilities' standards—it was twice as big as lavatories on domestic flights. But Colin Cannon's big body took up most of it. He leaned against the side wall studying her with those incredible green eyes. Did he wonder what kind of a woman would do this?

A woman like her, she realized. She stood rigid, holding her bag with a white-knuckled grip as she waited for him to move, to talk, to breathe. The space felt insular with the hum of the plane vibrating all around them.

He straightened and reached past her to lock the door, then took the bag and set it on a shelf, out of the way.

"I've never done anything like this before," she said.

"Neither have I," he said, then lifted his hand to her cheek. "You're beautiful." His voice had turned low and husky. "I didn't know if you'd come."

"I didn't know, either," she admitted. "I'm still not sure why I did."

"Then we're equally puzzled by one another." He lifted her chin and lowered his mouth to hers.

Zoe waited for the shock to her system, having another man's mouth on hers, but the only shock she had was how good it felt, how sensual. He kissed her thoroughly, cupping her face with both hands and delving deep with his strong tongue. She heard a moaning sound and realized it was her. Her hands, too, seemed disembodied. They slid up his chest, across the crisp fabric of his dress shirt, unfastening any buttons they encountered.

He smoothed his hands down her back and pulled her pelvis against his. The burn of his erection through the thin fabric of their clothes flipped some kind of carnal switch in Zoe. Heat flooded her body, she became feverish. Her breasts ached for his touch, her sex throbbed. She wanted his body sliding against hers…inside her.

Her sweater and bra went first, then his tie and shirt, then her panty hose and panties, then his belt. She released his bulging sex and sucked in an appreciative breath at the size of him. When she clasped the length of him, his eyes closed and he groaned with pleasure. He fumbled in his back pocket for a wallet and pulled out a condom.

"It's the only one I have," he murmured. "Let's make it last."

Zoe rolled it on and felt her body readying itself for him…warming, opening, expanding. He kissed her again, hungrily, nipping and licking. When he caught one nipple between his teeth and clamped down, she let him know she enjoyed the flash of pleasure-pain by squeezing his cock. "Now," she whispered.

He turned her around to face the mirror and kissed her neck while watching her reaction in the mirror. Then he removed the pins holding her hair and loosened it to lay in waves around her shoulders. "Look at you," he said near her ear, then tugged the lobe with his teeth.

Zoe almost didn't recognize herself. Her cheeks were flushed, her mouth bruised and open. Her eyes were nearly closed. She looked wanton, sexy…and thoroughly aroused.

He cupped her heavy breasts, brown fingers against the pale globes, and twisted the tips until they were distended. Lust like she'd never experienced coursed through her body. She thought she might faint from wanting him. She undulated her hips against his erection, and wanted her skirt to be gone. But when she reached for her hem, he clasped her hands and held them over her head.

"Soon," he murmured, "but not yet."

Holding both her hands with one of his, he wrapped his silk tie around her wrists again and again, then fashioned a loose knot. She could've gotten away if she wanted to, she thought distantly, but she didn't want to. As he held her hands against the coolness of the mirror, he worked magic on her body with the other hand, lifting her skirt and reaching around to stroke her slick folds and massage her clit. Zoe moaned and writhed against him, urging him with her body to take her. But he seemed determined to torture her with pleasure.

He worked her clit and kissed her neck, watching her all the while. His eyes, his hands, his body... God, she thought she might explode. A vibration deep in her womb was wending its way to the surface, but too slowly. She ground herself against his fingers to hasten the release and at last, a fierce orgasm claimed her. He kissed her, absorbing her cries.

Zoe was vaguely glad that one of them had the presence of mind to keep from drawing attention to their cubicle. She seemed unable to think at the moment, unable to do anything but feel…feel the numbing in her hands from the constriction of the tie, feel the edge of the sink as it cut into the front of her thighs, feel the pressure of his big body against hers. She knew the length of him would stretch her limits. She was weak with wanting him inside her.

And despite his promise to make her wait, she could tell by the clench of his hands and the set of his jaw that he, too, was nearing his breaking point. She spread her legs wider and thrust back against him, impaling herself on the head of his cock. A guttural noise escaped him, and on their next breath, he filled her completely.

Zoe's knees buckled from the sensory overload, but she leaned into the mirror and concentrated on keeping her eyes open. She wanted to see his face while he made love to her.

He was a beautiful man. His arms were long and muscular, his chest broad and covered with light hair. His face was ruggedly handsome and surprisingly expressive. From the pleasure playing over his face, he was enjoying the sex at least half as much as she was. Pure feminine satisfaction flooded her body as she met his long strokes, contracting her internal muscles around him. Not being able to use her hands helped her focus on other parts of her body—her nipples seemed ultrasensitive, and in this position, he seemed to be hitting a sweet spot…

Zoe came again, this orgasm more sudden and

more intense. He put his arm in front of her mouth and she bit down to smother her cries. He buried his face in her hair, then climaxed with a powerful contraction of his hips. His muffled groan reverberated in her ear. In that moment, she felt utterly sated.

He pulsed inside her for a long minute, allowing them both to recover. Then he gently unwound his tie from her wrists and helped to retrieve stray pieces of clothing. Zoe covered her breasts with her sweater and combed her hair back from her face with her hand. "I'd like to stay and freshen up."

He nodded and shrugged into his dress shirt, buttoning it and tucking it in with practiced ease. "Sure thing. By the way, that was amazing," he said matter-of-factly as he threaded his belt through the loops of his slacks.

She was staggered at how relaxed they both were, and conceded that not nearly enough oxygen had fully returned to her brain. The incident certainly qualified as mind-blowing.

He looped the wrinkled tie around his neck and fashioned a loose Windsor knot. "Can I see you again?"

Zoe blinked in surprise—she hadn't seen that coming. She'd just assumed that he was a traveling businessman looking for a quickie. In fact, she hadn't believed him when he'd said he'd never done this before. But no matter what his motivation or his circumstances, she couldn't ignore her own. "No, that's not possible. I'm—" she held up her left hand and her diamond engagement ring twinkled back "—I'm getting married in a month."

"Ah, I see," he said with a little smile that hinted of disappointment.

"I don't regret what happened," she said. "I wanted it, too. But I'm sure you understand why it has to end here."

"I do," he said, then winked. "I guess that's the groom's line, though, isn't it?"

She winced, then nodded. Her mind flashed to the black velvet ring box in Colin's jacket pocket, but she didn't mention it—she wasn't even supposed to know it was there.

"Too bad," he said, washing his hands in the sink and taking a minute to splash water on his face. For some reason, watching him wash up somehow seemed more intimate than what they had just shared. "It would've been a good time," he said, tossing the paper towels in the trash. He stopped, his hand on the doorknob, his green eyes lit with renewed cheer. "Good luck, Zoe."

"Thank you," she said, feeling awkard for the first time since their encounter.

He started to say something, then changed his mind. His white upper teeth sank into his lower lip. "He's a lucky bloke," he said finally, then left and closed the door behind him.

Zoe locked the door, then leaned into the sink to face herself in the mirror. She looked as if she'd been ridden hard...and had enjoyed it. Shame mixed with remorse started a slow drip as Kevin, whose face she could barely visualize before, now seemed branded on her mind. He would feel so betrayed if he knew what she'd done…and how good it had felt.

So she would never tell him. She'd had her little fling with a man who made her knees weak and had even gotten a taste of light bondage. It was over…done. Now she could move forward with the life she and Kevin had planned together and wouldn't have to wonder what she'd missed out on.

Can I see you again?

Moving quickly lest someone became suspicious of how long the bathroom had been occupied, she ran water in the sink and freshened up, then changed out of her uniform and into clothes that would travel well to the resort where she was staying in Sydney. Finally she rewound her hair into a thick knot at the nape of her neck.

Can I see you again?

When she emerged from the lavatory, passengers were beginning to rouse from their sleep. Light seeped into the cabin from windows that had been raised a few inches. She felt self-conscious as she made her way back to her seat, but no one seemed to know that she'd just had slam sex in the bathroom with a stranger.

Can I see you again?

Erica was awake and frowned at Zoe's new outfit. They rarely changed clothes before leaving the plane. Zoe gave Erica a little wave that she hoped came off as casual before reclaiming her seat. But once she was settled, her gaze kept straying to the curtain that divided coach from first class.

Can I see you again?

"It wouldn't work," she murmured.

"Did you say something?" the funky black-haired woman sitting next to her asked.

Zoe turned. The woman's eyes were indeed violet. How strange. Perhaps they were contact lenses. "No. I…was talking to myself."

"Helpful habit," the woman said with a smile. "It's amazing what you can talk yourself into."

"Or out of," Zoe added ruefully.

"Careful with that one," the woman said. "There are always plenty of people around who are more than happy to talk you out of doing things. Don't jump on the bandwagon."

Zoe smiled. "I'm Zoe. Is this your first trip to Australia?"

"I'm Lillian, and yes, it is. I can't wait to experience everything. You've probably been here dozens of times."

"Several," Zoe admitted. "This is my last trip, though. I'm transferring to a domestic route so that I can be home more. I'm getting married soon."

"Oh, how lovely."

"Yes," Zoe said, hoping she sounded more excited to the woman than she sounded to herself.

"So this is your last hurrah as a single woman?" her companion teased.

"Something like that," Zoe admitted.

"And afterward, maybe you can have that reunion with your old friend who wrote the letter."

Zoe nodded and smiled politely, but she knew that married Zoe would have to say goodbye forever to the Zoe who had written about her fantasies. Still, the letter had been the catalyst to indulging in the tryst in the lavatory. She had good memories to take home, something exciting to think about when she closed her eyes…

She did manage to doze off for a little while, and then they were landing.

"Why did you change clothes?" Erica asked when they met at the gate inside the terminal.

"I spilled red wine on my sweater," Zoe lied, rolling her suitcase toward customs and the exit. With their airline identification, they breezed through. She didn't see Colin Cannon, but then being a native, he would've gone through a different line. As they walked by baggage claim, she couldn't resist glancing over to see if she could spot him one last time.

"Who are you looking for?" Erica asked suspiciously.

"Er…the woman who sat next to me was so nice, I thought I'd wave goodbye if I saw her."

"Hurry, let's get a taxi. I can't wait to check out the resort."

Zoe followed her friend, feeling wistful as the taxi pulled away from the curb, leaving the airport behind. She would likely never see Colin again.

Which was just as well. She sat back in her seat and chewed on her thumbnail.

Erica nodded to the binder peeking out of Zoe's

bag. "I hope you're not going to worry about the wedding the entire time you're here."

"I won't, I promise. I just need to send a few e-mails to tie up loose ends."

"As long as you don't change your mind about the bridesmaids' dresses. Because I'm *so* looking forward to wearing what you've picked out. Did you say that strange color is apricot?"

Zoe winced apologetically. "My mother's idea."

"It's okay. I have one of those, too. I remember how she was when I planned my wedding."

Zoe nodded. It was as if her mother was determined that her daughter would have the wedding that she herself had always wanted. Satin and bows, lace and frippery. Which now seemed totally incongruous. Because after her encounter with Colin Cannon, all she could think about was leather and metal.

She gave herself a mental shake. Getting back into the details of the wedding would help to get her mind back where it belonged—on her groom.

Can I see you again?

Zoe forced the images of Colin from her head and concentrated on the view outside the taxi window. To her, Sydney was a cross between New York and San Francisco—bustling with people and cars, but hemmed by a breathtaking blue-and-white harbor. The resort was settled a few blocks from the epicenter of the city, in an older part of town. Its spalike atmosphere was a favorite destination for flight attendants, but the steep rates had always been a little pricey for Zoe. This was her first visit. Erica would be staying for two nights before returning to the States, but Zoe had used all her accumulated credit card points and splurged for ten days.

The lobby was soaring and lush with green plants and water features. The check-in process was smooth and quiet, their bags whisked away by white-suited bellmen.

"I'm going to need a nap before we do anything," Erica said, yawning.

"You go ahead," Zoe said. "The signal on my cell phone is strong. I'm going to try to reach Kevin and check e-mail. I'll be right up."

Erica nodded, her eyes drooping, then walked toward the elevator. Zoe moved to a quiet corner and pulled up her e-mail on her phone. She winced. Six messages from her mother, and from the subject lines, all of them had something to do with changes to the reception dinner seating chart, which Zoe was supposed to be working on.

Postponing reading them until later, she switched to phone mode and punched in Kevin's number. She desperately needed to talk to him, but considering it was almost midnight in Atlanta, she didn't expect him to answer. He usually went to bed early so he'd be rested for his morning workouts. When his voice-mail service kicked on, she felt a pang at the warm familiarity of his voice.

"Hi, it's me," she said brightly. "The flight was—"

traitorous "—fine. I'm—" *a big, fat cheater* "—fine."
Zoe pressed her lips together, telling herself she
needed to act as if everything was normal. As if she
wasn't still tender in places from being with another
man, as if she wasn't still besieged by images of
them together. "I'll call you later. Bye." It was only
after she hung up that she realized she hadn't said
that she loved him.

And the guilt that she'd been expecting finally
swamped her body with the force of a flash flood.
She closed her eyes against the physical pain until it
ebbed, then told herself that there was nothing left
to do but to live with it.

She turned to face the expansive white lobby,
enjoying the peaceful chiming sounds of Aboriginal
music playing overhead. Sun poured in on the
gleaming floor tile and polished brass fixtures.
Overhead fans stirred the branches of potted fig
trees. She inhaled deeply and exhaled, feeling instantly calmer. This soothing ambience was exactly
what she needed to relax and to rid her mind of one
Colin Cannon.

"This is a nice surprise."

Zoe pivoted to see the man himself standing at the
check-in desk, a duffel in one hand, a briefcase in the
other. His leather duster nearly touched the ground.
Her mouth opened and closed as alarms sounded in
her head. When the shock subsided, disbelief and
anger set in.

She strode up to him, her heart racing double-time. "Mr. Cannon," she said, trying to keep her voice calm, "what happened on the plane was a one-time thing. You had no right to follow me here."

He looked confused, then smiled. "I didn't follow you here, Zoe. This is purely a coincidence."

That was possible, she conceded. "Th-then you'll have to go to another hotel."

"That would be rather difficult," he said.

Zoe crossed her arms. "Why?"

Colin was interrupted by a reservations employee who handed him a flat wooden box over the counter. "Your keys, Mr. Cannon. I'll ring the bellman."

He thanked the woman, then turned back to Zoe, taking in her belligerent stance with an amused expression. "Because...I happen to own this place."

4

AT THE NEWS THAT SHE'D just checked in to a resort owned by the man with whom she'd gotten down and dirty in the airplane lavatory, Zoe's mind whirled in confusion. Followed by bleeding mortification that she'd just accused Colin Cannon of stalking her.

She blinked and her mouth gaped. "I…I…"

A smile crept across his handsome face as he gestured to the incredibly lavish lobby—*his* lobby. "Thank you. This place renders me speechless sometimes, too. That's why I bought it." Then he leaned in close to her ear and murmured, "My apologies. If I'd known we were bound for the same destination, I would've postponed my invitation until we were in more comfortable quarters."

Zoe swallowed hard. "Let's just forget about it, okay?"

"Too late," he said. "You left an indelible impression."

So had he, she conceded. His close proximity gave her a whiff of the cologne she had smelled on his neck. And he was still wearing the silk tie that had bound her wrists, now neatly reknotted at his shirt collar. Zoe took a step backward to clear her head.

"I'm moving to another hotel," she announced.

His face creased in disappointment. "Please don't. It's a big resort, our paths probably won't even cross. Are you a regular guest?"

"No," she said, then gave him a wry frown. "No offense, but it's a little beyond my normal budget. But a co-worker and I are here for—" she swallowed the real reason "—a treat."

"Ah," he said. "A prewedding treat?"

She nodded, awash with shame.

"Then a treat you shall have," he said with a wink. He turned back to the reservations desk. "Please arrange for Ms. Smythe and—" He looked back to Zoe. "What is your friend's name?"

"Erica Winston."

He nodded to the clerk. "Please arrange for Ms. Smythe and Ms. Winston to have complimentary use of our spa during their stay."

"Very good, sir," the woman responded.

"That's not necessary," Zoe said, feeling flushed all over again.

"It's my pleasure," Colin said, his green eyes reflecting something akin to regret. "Enjoy your stay, Zoe." Then, with a little salute, he strode away.

She watched his broad back receding, feeling shaky, as if she had just averted disaster. She exhaled slowly and hugged herself for extra assurance that she wasn't coming apart at the seams. Everything was fine, she told herself. The man seemed content to forget about their impromptu encounter and, in fact, seemed eager to offer inducements for her to forget, too. It was probably just another in a long line of hookups for him, she realized. He wouldn't understand that for her, the incident had been a lapse of monumental proportions, one that would be harder to forget knowing that he, too, was staying at the resort.

On the other hand, what explanation could she give to Erica for changing hotels? They'd both been looking forward to this getaway. And now, with unlimited use of the spa…

No, she'd stay put, at least until Erica left in two days. Then she'd take stock of the situation. Like Colin said, the resort was a big place—he and she might never cross paths.

With her mind still clicking away, it was clear that the nap she had promised herself was not to be. Instead she shouldered her bag and exited the hotel, blinking in the bright sunshine. Knowing how brutal the Australian sun could be, she smeared on sunscreen and purchased a wide-brim hat at the first shop she came to. It was fall in the States, but spring had sprung here on the lower side of the equator, and it was surprisingly warm considering the proximity of the bay waters.

Zoe wandered the streets looking for eclectic jewelry stores, as she did at each travel destination, searching for beads, stones and other materials for her jewelry-making hobby. Australia was known for its amazing opals and she'd decided they would be perfect accent stones for the silver link bracelets she was making as gifts for her bridesmaids.

The task also put her mind back where it belonged—on her future, on her wedding—while she soaked up the atmosphere of the harbor city. The tang of salt rode the air, along with the sounds of the accents of the people strolling by, going about their day.

Zoe loved to catch hints of their conversation— the way the words seemed to roll together with a buoyant rhythm that told anyone listening that Australians were generally a happy and upbeat people. Greetings among friends were exuberant, backslapping events with raised voices and broad smiles. The common phrase of "no worries" summed up the people's sunny attitude.

She walked into shops and browsed bins of trinkets. Intrigued by colorful Aboriginal clay beads, she purchased several to make something for herself at a later date. The selection of opal jewelry was extensive, as were the range of hues of the distinctive stones—from pale and milky to dark and vibrant, each alight with fiery specks of color. When she didn't find any loose stones, however, she gave up the search for another day. Conceding to her growling stomach, Zoe bought a fish sandwich at a concession stand near Circular Quay and walked to the pier surrounding Sydney Cove to have lunch.

Sydney Harbour was one of the greatest tourist attractions in the country, although the locals also hung out there, obviously drawn to the cobalt-blue water and the buzz of activity. The famous white-winged Sydney Opera House was in easy viewing and walking distance to her right—she had endured the long lines and toured it on a previous trip to Sydney. The Harbour Bridge ascended to her left. If she squinted, she could make out the slow-moving train of ants on the arch, high above traffic and the harbor, that were actually people braving the famous Sydney BridgeClimb.

Along the Circular Quay pier, upscale restaurants and shops amiably shared space with street vendors and picnic tables. Fat pigeons and gulls flocked at the feet of diners, poised to dive on falling crumbs. Boats of all sizes were docked at the marina—runabouts, sailboats and ferries. But many of the slips were empty on this sunny, breezy day, further evidenced by the bobbing dots on the near and far horizons.

Leaning against a white railing and slowly chewing the sandwich, Zoe detected a subtle change in her senses as they became more keen. Everything around her seemed to be in sharper focus, more vivid, more apparent. Boat horns sounded a symphony as they entered and left the harbor. Water lapped against the pier in a whispering caress. Children's screams of laughter pierced the air.

She could blame some of the insular wooziness on jet lag and lack of sleep, but deep down, as much as she was trying to push it out of her mind, the incident on the plane with Colin Cannon had heightened her self-awareness. The birds were singing, and so was her skin where he'd touched her. The surf was pounding, and so was her pulse when she remembered the way he'd looked at her. The sky soared overhead, and so did her imagination when she dared to think about what it might be like to spend an entire night in his arms…under his tutelage.

This sense of wonder at the pure intensity that could exist between two people—she'd never felt anything like it before. It was as if a veil had been lifted from her eyes, and she couldn't believe she'd lived this long and not known. She wasn't a sheltered person—at least she'd never thought so. She stared at her engagement ring and acknowledged the truth—since she'd met Kevin, she'd systematically tucked in all the edges of her adventurous spirit, preparing to settle down, to raise a family, to grow old. The evolution was a natural part of growing up, wasn't it? And it had happened so slowly, she hadn't even noticed.

Which was why she felt so blindsided by her encounter with Colin Cannon. The incident was like catching lightning in a bottle, she decided—coming into contact with the right person at the right time, when both of them were in the right mood. Pent-up…unfulfilled…searching. Odds were that it would never happen again, not with him, not with anyone. It was a fluke.

Zoe tossed the rest of her sandwich to the birds and watched them devour it. The pure hunger in

Colin Cannon's eyes had been just as animalistic. His primitive desires had driven her to do things that she hadn't thought about in years.

Until the letter arrived.

She reached into her bag and removed the envelope, turning it over and over. How uncanny that it had shown up just before her wedding. Although she did recall Dr. Alexander saying that in ten years' time, when most of the senior girls would be thirty-two years old, they would likely be at pivotal points in their lives, on the verge of marriage or having children or even divorcing. It was the perfect time for reevaluation, Dr. Alexander had said. Just as their bodies were speeding toward a sexual peak.

Zoe lifted a hand to her flushed cheek. Was that why she'd reacted so fiercely to the Aussie, because more potent hormones were pumping through her body? Was it nature's way of telling her to have fun before it was too late? Before she settled down?

She shoved the letter back into her bag. This wasn't the kind of conversation she thought she'd be having with herself on this trip. The layover was supposed to be a time to catch her breath before the whirlwind of the wedding, a time to anticipate starting her life with Kevin.

Not to have an illicit encounter with a stranger. Just because he was broad shouldered and blond and wealthy and sexy and older and Australian—as opposite of Kevin as possible. And on the opposite side of the world.

A tall figure strolling across the boardwalk toward the marina caught her eye and she inhaled sharply. It was Colin Cannon, and he noticed her at the same time. He was dressed in khaki cargo shorts, a navy Windbreaker and faded deck shoes, carrying a small duffel bag. He was obviously headed to a boat—to *his* boat, no doubt. Still several yards away, he lifted his hand in a friendly wave.

Zoe didn't react, at least, not outwardly. But seeing him again sent all kinds of carnal thoughts spiraling through her head. Snatches of their time together came back in vivid detail—seeing his face next to hers in the mirror as he made love to her from behind, holding her bound wrists overhead. She felt faint with sensory overload and reached out to touch the rail in front of her, to ground herself. She needed sleep, she reasoned. She was exhausted, her defenses were down. Once she got the rest she needed and the relaxation she'd come here for, she'd be better equipped to deal with what had happened, better able to resist Colin if their paths crossed again.

He hesitated, then made a move in her direction.

Zoe turned and walked as fast as she could away from him, back toward the resort. She felt his gaze on her and realized with dismay that she wasn't running away from Colin Cannon as much as she was running away from her own weaknesses.

Because she didn't trust herself around him.

5

<hr/>

"ZOE, WHAT'S WRONG?" Erica said in a muffled voice.

In the next mud tub over, Zoe's eyelids were pleasantly weighted with cool chamomile tea bags, her face wrapped with a warm, moist towel. Only their swaddled heads extended from the black goo, and she desperately wanted to scratch her nose.

"Nothing's wrong," she responded. "Why do you think something's wrong?" From under the towel, her own voice sounded squeaky and high-pitched.

"I don't know, that's why I'm asking. You've been in a fog for two days. Is something bothering you?"

Zoe winced inwardly. So she hadn't been doing a very good job at hiding her stubborn preoccupation with Colin Cannon. She lifted a mud-covered hand from the bath and removed the warm towel and tea bags. "I just have a lot on my mind, that's all. I'm sorry. You were good enough to stay with me these two days and I haven't been very good company."

A laugh sounded from behind the towel. "Are you kidding? Jim and I needed a break from each other and this has been heaven. But I'm worried about you." Her covered head pivoted toward Zoe. "You're not getting cold feet about marrying Kevin, are you?"

Zoe's forced laugh came out sounding a little too much like machine-gun report. "Of course not." But she was glad that Erica couldn't see her face.

"Because if you are, now's the time to work it all out in your head." Then Erica gasped. "Oh, I forgot to tell you, I saw that man from the plane."

Zoe's heart jumped. "What man?"

"That hunky guy in first class that gave you the 'vibe,' remember?"

"Oh, yeah," Zoe said with a little chuckle.

"I saw him in the lobby this morning. He's walking around as if he owns the place."

"Good to know," Zoe said carefully. "So I can avoid him."

"Uh-huh," Erica said, then expelled a long, lazy sigh. "I'm going to miss this. I'd still like to know who you slept with to get us unlimited access to the spa."

Zoe swallowed nervously. "I told you. When I booked the rooms, I mentioned it was a prewedding getaway. The manager must have found out and decided to do something special."

"Well, it worked," Erica murmured. "I've never felt so pampered in my life. Is there any service we didn't get?"

"I don't think so," Zoe said. "Although I'm regretting the Brazilian bikini wax."

"The tenderness goes away," Erica assured her.

"Trust me, you're going to love it. Having sex with a Brazilian wax is amazing."

The wrong man's face and body came to mind, and Zoe nearly groaned aloud. "What time is your flight out in the morning?" she asked, changing the subject.

"Early. I'll try not to wake you when I leave. Do you have big plans tomorrow?"

"I might take a walk through the Royal Botanic Gardens. And I'd like to get to Manly Beach before I leave." Maybe the time alone would clear her head.

"That sounds nice," Erica agreed. "Have you talked to Kevin?"

"No, we keep missing each other." That was part of the problem, she told herself. Talking to her fiancé would crowd Colin Cannon out of her head, but when he wasn't traveling with his sports-equipment sales job, Kevin was spending every free minute training on his bike. They were even honeymooning Stateside, so he could take his racing cycle along. Boulder, Colorado, was a beautiful city, she conceded. She didn't mind that it was also one of the best places in the country for long-distance training.

Really, she didn't.

On Erica's last night they decided to take in a music festival at the harbor. They drank beer and moved from stage to stage listening to everything ranging from the pulsating vibrations of Aboriginal music to the throbbing beat of full-on rock and roll. The weather was balmy and the heaving crowd was festive.

Zoe was glad for the noise and the activity because she didn't have to make conversation. But the constant thump of the music resonated through her body, playing on sensitive nerve endings, bringing to mind a different kind of rhythm. Lubricated with alcohol, she and Erica swayed and danced with the masses. Zoe felt languid and weightless, enjoying the high from the strong beer and the energy from the bodies around them.

"Don't look now," Erica shouted in her ear, "but there's your hunky Aussie!"

Still moving to the beat of the music from the nearest stage, Zoe nonchalantly turned around and sure enough, Colin Cannon stood a few feet away, watching her with hooded green eyes. He wasn't standing apart from the crowd, but to her, he was impossible to miss. His rugged body was dressed in jeans and a white button-up shirt. His bronzed skin glowed with vitality, his sun-kissed hair rumpled and sexy.

Just knowing he was nearby sent the thrum of the bass to her sex…*boom…boom…boom.* Zoe continued to undulate to the music, moving her shoulders and hips in a slow shimmy, holding her arms over her head. A delicious shudder ran up her spine as he devoured her with his gaze. This was safe, she told herself. He could watch her and she could enjoy having him watch her without anything happening. She had Erica as her insurance tonight.

Erica is leaving tomorrow, her mind whispered.

Ignoring the nagging voice in her head, Zoe

turned away from him, moving in slow, erotic circles. The men around her howled and made suggestive comments, but she was dancing only for Colin. When she'd come full circle, she looked up…but he was gone. Disappointment flooded her chest as she scanned the area, but she chastised herself, embarrassed at her behavior. She'd made it clear that she wasn't going to pick up where they'd left off. And it looked as if he intended to respect her wishes.

Zoe sighed. Apparently he was a gentleman.

"I don't think you've seen the last of him," Erica said in her ear.

Zoe waved off her friend, pretending that she didn't know what Erica was talking about. The rest of the evening held less interest for her, but she stayed until Erica was ready to leave. And Erica was determined to make the most of her last night of freedom. Her friend flirted and danced dirty with more than one guy, but ultimately turned down their end-of-the-evening invitations. Despite all her grousing about her sex-starved marriage, Erica didn't appear to be looking for an affair.

"Let's go," she said around two in the morning. "I have to leave in a few hours and get back to reality."

Zoe linked arms with her friend as they made the short walk back to the hotel. "Admit it, you miss Jim, don't you?"

"Yes," Erica said, her voice slurred and wistful. "Jim doesn't burn up the sheets, but he rubs my feet and makes me laugh. That's what's important, isn't it?"

"Yes," Zoe agreed.

"Besides, it's too much to expect to have it all with one person—great sex *and* great love, right?"

"Right," Zoe agreed, although Dr. Alexander had said quite the opposite in her Sex for Beginners class. Zoe's mind and body were still buzzing from the earlier appearance—then disappearance—of Colin Cannon. The man pulled on her body's rhythms like a cosmic force.

The temperature had grown cooler, so she hurried Erica along the cobbled streets to the hotel. Inside, she scanned the lobby, hoping for a glimpse of the owner, but only a few employees were on duty at this hour. When they arrived at their room, Erica phoned for a wake-up call and fell onto her bed in an immediate deep sleep.

Zoe, on the other hand, lay on her bed fully dressed. She stared at the ceiling, trying to sort through why she felt so muddled and restless, why her mind kept ping-ponging back and forth between two men, when one of them had stepped out of the picture—at her request. She felt torn and confused and angry at herself for doing something to jeopardize her feelings for Kevin.

Across the room, her cell phone rang, glowing in the darkness of the room. Zoe hurried to answer it so the noise wouldn't disturb Erica. Kevin's name and number flashed on the screen. She closed her eyes briefly before answering. "Hello?"

"Hi, Zoe. It's me. Did I wake you?"

"Actually, no." She slipped her feet into her shoes,

grabbed her room key and headed out into the hallway in search of a quiet area where she could talk.

"Still getting used to the time change, huh?"

"Right," she said, walking toward a sofa situated near the elevator. "How are you?" It was just after noon in Atlanta; he would be on his lunch break.

"Great," he said, his voice jovial, as always. "I had a good ride yesterday. The new shoe clips make all the difference."

"That's nice," she said, trying to work up some enthusiasm for his consuming pastime. After all, it would soon be a big part of her life, too.

"So how about you? Have you been doing anything fun?"

She winced as "fun" images of her and another man came to mind. "Oh, yeah, Erica and I have been practically living in the spa."

"She leaves today, doesn't she?"

"In a few hours."

"Gee, won't you be lonely?"

"No," she assured him, and to her dismay, once again Colin's face popped into her head. "I'm looking forward to some quiet time."

"I hate to bring it up, but my mother called again about the seating chart for the reception. My aunt Lynn and my aunt Marion are fighting, so they can't sit at the same table."

Zoe put her hand to her temple. Oh, yeah—the wedding. "Okay. I'll see what I can do."

"Oh, and I found out that the Olympic cycling team will be performing time trials while we're in Boulder. Isn't that great?"

"That's great," she agreed. *Kevin, how about riding me as hard as you ride that bike of yours?* She swallowed the facetious words and instead said, "Hope we won't be too tied up to enjoy our honeymoon." *Tied up.* She groaned inwardly at the slip of her tongue.

"No way," Kevin said easily. "It's going to be a fantastic trip. By the way, I moved your kitchen table and chairs to my place."

"Thanks," she said, thinking how comfortably they moved in and around each other. They had decided to live in his small house and save money for something larger. Kevin had begun moving things from her apartment little by little. It was natural...so why did it suddenly bother her? Why did it feel as if he was encroaching, that she was being absorbed into his life?

"I have to run, Zoe, but it's good to hear your voice. I don't want you to forget about me while you're on the other side of the world."

She tried to match his light tone. "Not a chance."

"Talk to you soon?"

"Absolutely."

"I love you, Zoe."

"I...love you, too." She disconnected the call and leaned her head back on the sofa, soaking in the silence of the hotel hallway. Why was she suddenly questioning everything she had thought to be right?

Too wide-awake to return to her room, she pushed to her feet and punched the elevator call button. After stepping inside, she scanned the floor directory and remembered the hotel had a rooftop garden. It sounded like a nice place to clear her head. Zoe punched the button to take her to the top of the hotel and listened to the chime as she ascended each floor.

When the car stopped and the elevator doors opened, a cool breeze blew across her face, lifting her hair off her neck. Stepping across the threshold, Zoe inhaled the scent of moss and earth and gasped at the almost magical quality of the garden at this quiet hour. Lanterns hanging from shepherds' hooks illuminated the area, made up of plants, trees and flowers in containers and in box beds created from tiered timbers. A chest-high wall surrounded the rooftop oasis.

She walked over to take in the view, enchanted by the panorama of twinkling lights from the Harbour Bridge, the water and surrounding buildings. All was quiet, bound up in sleep. The predawn horizon was a clear dark teal, hinting at a beautiful day to come. Zoe crossed her arms against the chill, feeling blessed, as if the scene was hers alone to savor.

The sound of a small fountain bubbling led her away from the wall and into the garden, toward one of several benches faintly illuminated by underlighting. The aroma of a cigar reached her just as the glow of an ash appeared. Realizing she wasn't alone, she murmured, "Pardon me," and turned to go.

"Don't leave, Zoe," a man's voice said.

A familiar voice. One that caused her vital signs to go haywire.

"Colin, is that you?" She stared until she could make out his large frame sprawled on the bench.

"Yes. My body hasn't yet adjusted to the time change. For some reason, this time it's worse than usual." His disembodied voice rolled over her, richly accented. *Strine,* as Australians would say.

"I know what you mean," she confessed.

"Come sit with me."

"I shouldn't—"

"Please. Help me figure this out."

Compelled, she edged closer and felt her way to the bench, lowering herself gingerly. Their knees brushed as she sat back, sending vibrations through her midsection. Her eyes quickly acclimated to the dark. She could see his face and noticed that he was wearing the same clothes he'd worn earlier, when he'd watched her dance. Her heart thudded in her chest. "Figure what out?"

He took his time snuffing the cigar in some kind of container. "This…attraction between us," he said finally, sounding perplexed. "Don't get me wrong, you're an exceptionally beautiful woman. But I've known lots of beautiful women and none of them have made me lose my appetite or zone out during a business meeting." He moved closer and suddenly his mouth was near her ear. "Did you cast some kind of spell on me?"

She laughed softly at his remark, even as desire surged through her body. "No," she managed to say.

"I want you again, Zoe."

His simple statement was a blow to her resolve. "But I'm—"

"Getting married soon, I heard that part. But you're not married yet."

His hoarse whisper was more like a challenge, sending a shiver of longing over her shoulders.

"Have you and your friend enjoyed your visits to the spa?"

"Yes," she said breathlessly. "Th-thank you for the special attention."

"I noticed your friend is checking out tomorrow."

"That's right," she murmured.

"But you're staying for a few more days."

Her mind raced. She had told herself she might look for another hotel when Erica left, just to put some space between her and this man. But at this moment, she couldn't think of why she'd want to be away from him. "Yes."

Colin put his mouth close to hers. "Excellent." He didn't kiss her, but his lips caressed hers as he rasped, "I'm in the penthouse, room 1200. If you change your mind and want some *truly* special attention, knock on my door."

Then he pushed to his feet and walked away.

6

ZOE RETURNED TO HER ROOM in a daze, Colin's provocative invitation swirling through her head. Her
body was exhausted, but her mind wouldn't allow
her to fall asleep for a long while. She lay in the dark
replaying the words he'd said over and over.

*I want you again, Zoe. I want you again... I want
you again...*

*I'm in the penthouse... If you change your mind and
want some truly special attention, knock on my door.*

She wasn't sure exactly what he'd meant, but it
sounded...intriguing. Still, she shouldn't take him up
on his offer...she couldn't...

When she finally dozed off, Zoe slept fitfully,
plagued by troublesome images of Kevin and Colin
and herself. She was in her bridal gown, running, but
away from something or toward something, she
couldn't tell. And then she felt as if she were walking
in quicksand—her feet were moving, but she wasn't
going anywhere. Frustration rose in her chest until she
cried out.

Zoe jerked awake, her mouth dry and her legs

tangled in the sheets. Daylight streamed in around the curtains and Erica was gone, with a note left on her pillow that read "Do everything I wouldn't do."

Zoe groaned—it was a conspiracy. She pushed her hand into her hair and picked up the tableside clock. It was already midmorning. She needed to take a shower and get moving, needed to do something to take her mind off Colin Cannon and his outrageous proposition. Working out the details of her upcoming wedding should do the trick.

The shower and a couple of aspirin did revive her somewhat and helped to clear her mind. After all, just because an impossibly sexy man had invited her to indulge in a few days of illicit sex, didn't mean she was going to do it.

She dressed in comfortable clothes, put the "Zoe and Kevin's Wedding" binder in her bag and left the hotel, walking briskly while glancing out from under the brim of her hat for any sign of Colin. She didn't encounter him and breathed a little easier when she reached the street.

Just because she hadn't instantly rejected him didn't mean she was actually considering it.

It was another beautiful day with mild temperatures and sun, sun, sun. Zoe walked to the Royal Botanic Gardens by way of the southern end of Circular Quay, past the Opera House. Sydney Harbour jutted a deep C into the gardens, but a walkway next to the water was one of the most popular attractions. Zoe bought a chicken kebob and a bottle of water at a vendor cart and ate as she strolled. But even in the midst of the burgeoning lunch crowd picnicking in clumps on the expansive grassy inclines, she felt singular and alone.

At the section of the gardens where the harbor cut the deepest, Zoe left the walkway and wandered past the spectacular Oriental garden to seek out her favorite spot, the Palm Grove. The shady haven included the garden's oldest trees, some of them more than one hundred fifty years old. On her many trips to Sydney, she always made a point to bring a book to enjoy in the grove. This time she chose a particularly beautiful cabbage palm and settled near the trunk before pulling out the wedding binder.

Zoe stared at it hard, trying to recapture the enthusiasm she'd felt when her mother had first handed her the binder, saying they were going to have to be ultraorganized to make sure everything went smoothly. She opened the book and ran her fingers over the color-coded tabs. Her mother had handled most of the big details—securing the church, the minister, the reception hall, the photographer, the videographer, the florist, the caterer.

Her mother had even chosen the wedding gown, although Zoe did love it. The bridesmaids' dresses were another matter, she thought with a laugh. She would've chosen a color other than apricot. But her mother had convinced her that the shade would be lovely in the photos. And since her parents were footing the bill for most of the expenses, she felt obligated to defer to her mother's judgment. Her marriage to Kevin was the only thing her parents seemed to agree on. It was a nice reprieve from the constant bickering.

With a sigh she downloaded her e-mail and grimaced to see more messages from her mother, all about the wedding. In her absence, her mother had chosen the decorations for the head tables, and had invited Kevin over for dinner so he could choose the music mix for the band.

It'll be one less thing for you to worry about, dear. Your father and I are so happy for you and Kevin. You know we love him like a son. Hope you're having fun on your last trip to Sydney.

Zoe bit into her lip. She was lucky that her parents approved of Kevin and that he got along so well with them—her engagement had had a calming effect on her parents' volatile relationship. Both her mother and father had commented on how congenial she and Kevin were. Zoe's hope was that she and Kevin would rub off on them. Ditto for Kevin's parents, who were like two birds pecking at each other.

Zoe sighed and unfolded the seating chart for the reception that still needed to be worked out. Twenty tables, ten persons per table, and countless conflicts. She put a mark through Kevin's aunt Marion and moved her to a table where she wouldn't be able to make eye contact with Aunt Lynn. But that displaced a co-worker of her mother's who might or might not be bringing a friend with her, which would leave the friend sitting alone…but would also give them the flexibility of moving everyone back if Aunt Marion and Aunt Lynn were suddenly on speaking terms again by the wedding.

And then she pulled up the e-mails from her mother:

Don't sit Susan Jennings with Tim Miltman—they're in litigation.

Randy Holder is a strict vegetarian and asked not to sit at the same table with big-game hunter Nolan Graham.

Karen and Darrell Williams are separating and no longer wish to sit together; in fact, seat them on opposite sides of the room and remove the steak knives from their place settings.

Lynda Samples asked if you could please sit her nephew Art Finnis next to an eligible young woman of good reputation.

Fiona Sites asked if she could be seated as close as possible to the restroom.

Brad Station asked if he could be seated as close as possible to the bar.

Please find a single person to sit between Mr. Dunbar and Mr. Wheaten at table five.

Zoe made a frustrated noise and lifted her hand to massage her temple.

"Hello, there."

She looked up to see a fortyish petite woman with a pink streak in her short black hair. It took a few seconds for Zoe to place her as the woman who had sat next to her on the plane, the one who'd asked about the letter she'd been reading. "Hi. Lillian, right?"

The woman smiled and nodded. "And you're Zoe?"

"Yes."

"I'm sorry, am I interrupting? I was on my way to the Tropical Centre to see the orchids and noticed you here."

"No—please, sit." Zoe closed the notebook. "Trust me, I'm happy for the diversion."

Lillian lowered herself to the grass near Zoe, then gestured to the binder. "Planning a wedding can be stressful."

Zoe sighed. "You can say that again. Everyone seems to think it's about them."

"Weddings do tend to bring out the best and worst in people. Is it going to be a big ceremony?"

"Bigger than I anticipated," Zoe admitted. "But my mother… Well, it'll be nice."

Lillian smiled wide. "I'm sure it will. Your ring is lovely."

Zoe glanced at her diamond engagement ring and

murmured her thanks. As a hobbyist jeweler, she would've chosen a nontraditional stone, something unique, if Kevin had consulted her. But he hadn't. Still, it was indeed a beautiful ring.

"What's your fiancé like?" the woman asked.

"Kevin? He's…a nice man."

"The two of you must be very compatible."

A vision of her and Kevin's *in*compatibility came to mind in the form of a tall, blond, green-eyed Aussie, and Zoe almost panicked—had Lillian seen Colin signal her on the plane to join him in the lavatory? Her throat closed as snatches of the two of them together bombarded her, along with his blatant suggestion last night that she "knock on his door." Zoe squirmed. Eager to change the subject, she asked, "So, how do you like Australia?"

"It's positively lovely." The woman's violet-colored eyes sparkled. "The people here are so friendly, and there's an economy to everything and everybody that's just so pleasing."

"I agree. I'm going to miss flying here."

"Where do you live?"

"Atlanta."

"What a coincidence, so do I. What part?"

"Downtown. How about you?"

"South of the airport," the woman said. "But I'm moving in a couple of months."

"Moving where?"

Lillian shrugged. "I'm not really sure yet. Wherever life takes me."

Zoe liked the woman's adventurous spirit. "Are you visiting other cities in Australia?"

Lillian nodded. "Melbourne and Cairns."

"I love Melbourne, and of course, you'll have to see the Great Barrier Reef."

"I can't wait." The woman glanced up as a broad-shouldered man walked by. A mischievous smile lit her face as she leaned in. "The country is beautiful, but I must say, so are the countrymen."

Zoe's mouth went dry. "Um…yes…I suppose."

Lillian leaned in. "What a lovely necklace."

"Thank you," Zoe said, toying with the beaded silver mesh that she'd braided herself. She was always shy of telling people that she made jewelry.

Lillian pushed to her feet. "Well, I've intruded on your quiet time long enough. It was nice to run into you."

"Same here," Zoe said. "When are you flying back?"

"Thursday, on the early flight."

"Me, too. Perhaps we'll see each other again."

"I'd like that," Lillian said, dusting grass off her jeans. "By the way, did you decide whether you're going to hook up with your old friend, the one who wrote the letter?"

Did she even want the opportunity to become re-acquainted with the sexually fearless woman she'd been when she'd written that letter? Zoe gave Lillian a wistful smile. "I'm starting to think that some things are better left alone."

A small furrow appeared between Lillian's eyebrows. "I'm sorry to hear that. But I'm sure you'll do what's best. Enjoy your vacation, Zoe. You have the rest of your life to be married."

Zoe lifted her hand in a wave as the attractive woman walked away, then frowned in puzzlement. What a strange thing to say....

She looked down at the binder and sighed. She had lost interest in working on the seating chart. She stowed it in her bag, then continued her stroll through the gardens. But even the view from Lady Macquarie's Chair, a seat for a former governor's wife, carved into the rock on the southernmost tip of the garden and overlooking the harbor, failed to take her mind off the conflict brewing inside her. If anything, staring out over the blue water made her feel even more restless.

Her body hummed with unspent energy. She was flushed and could tell her internal temperature had risen. She felt nervous and unsteady, as if the wind might pick her up and blow her across the harbor…to Colin? Even at this distance, she could feel the pull of him on her body. Was he sitting in a business meeting, distracted by the thought of her, wondering if she would take him up on his invitation?

She put her cool hand on the back of her heated neck and closed her eyes. Their sexual chemistry was undeniable, and admittedly, so was her curiosity. This might be her last chance to have her fantasies fulfilled before settling into the rest of her life. But deep down, she was afraid. Afraid that Colin

Cannon would awaken a hunger within her that would need constant feeding. The man had already commandeered her peace of mind.

On the other hand, the black velvet ring box in Colin's jacket pocket implied he was on the verge of settling down himself. Maybe this was also a chance for him to explore a few fantasies before he took his vows.

Nice try, Zoe...trying to rationalize a fling as a good deed.

She looked up into the afternoon sun that was already starting its slow descent. In a few hours it would be dusk, then darkness would settle. Time for bed.

Zoe fingered her engagement ring, pondering her intoxicating dilemma.

"MR. CANNON?"

Colin turned his head and realized that everyone in the boardroom was staring at him. "I'm sorry, mate, say again?"

Benjamin Rook stood and pulled at the waist of his pants. "Why don't we finish this up tomorrow, everyone?"

Colin sighed and nodded, supremely irritated with himself. While the meeting attendees gathered their notes and filed out, he shoved his notebook that contained little more than doodles back into his briefcase and snapped it shut.

Benjamin walked up. "You okay?"

Colin pulled his hand down his face. "Yeah, sorry. My concentration is off the mark."

"Something happen in Atlanta?"

"No, it was a good meeting. The property there looks very promising. The city is working on a beltline transportation project that will make it an even more desirable location in a few years' time. And now that the open-skies agreement has lifted restrictions on airlines traveling between here and the States, it makes sense for us to partner in this expansion."

Benjamin nodded. "I'm giving it every consideration. So, is something else bothering you? Is it Lauren?" He grinned. "I hear that my sister is pressuring you for a ring. High time that the two of you settled down, I say."

Colin pressed his lips together, wondering what his mate and business partner would think of him if he knew a slip of an American woman had him preoccupied. "Just having a harder time than usual adjusting to the time change."

His friend smiled as he shrugged into his jacket. "Okay, I'll see you tomorrow. Get some sleep tonight."

Colin nodded, lifting his hand, but when the door closed, he brought his hand down on the table with a thud. What a wanker he was being. Zoe Smythe had made it clear that what had happened on the plane was a one-time encounter. So why did he feel as if he would explode if he couldn't have her again? Over the years, many women had come and gone from his bed. Lauren Rook had been keeping him cozy for over a year and he'd grown very fond of her.

But there was something about this Zoe that spoke to him on such a base level, it was as if all the social sophistication he'd honed during his lifetime meant nothing. His reaction to her was purely instinctual…primitive, even. All he could think about was doing delicious things to her lithe body, to probe the depths of her pleasure. He'd noticed the way she'd reacted to having his tie binding her wrists. Was she up to something more extreme? Just thinking about tying her to his bed made his cock swell.

Then Colin scoffed. He'd most likely scared her off with his Neanderthal tactics. In fact, he'd be damn lucky if she didn't report him to his own hotel management. If so, he deserved it. The woman was getting married in a few weeks. If he had any integrity, he'd leave her the hell alone.

With a glance at his watch, he picked up his jacket and briefcase and left the boardroom of his office building. It was only a short drive to the hotel, but his temper was equally short as he maneuvered through rush hour. When he arrived at the entrance, he tossed the keys to the valet and strode inside, stopping at the front desk.

"G'day, Mr. Cannon," the clerk said crisply. "What can I do for you, sir?"

"G'day," he said absently, loosening his tie. "I'm

leaving for Canberra. Could you send a bellman to my room, please?"

"Yes, sir."

Colin turned toward the elevator. He'd have to get Benjamin to reschedule tomorrow's meeting. For now, the best thing to do was to get out of Sydney until one Miss Zoe Smythe was on her way back to Atlanta.

Feeling better having made the decision, he rode up to his penthouse room, left a message for Ben and opened the curtains to enjoy the panoramic view while he packed. He poured himself a vodka on the rocks from the wet bar and with the touch of a stereo remote control, coaxed the acoustic, eclectic music of The John Butler Trio from the ceiling speakers.

He pulled durable clothes from the walk-in robe and folded them hastily, stuffing them into two large leather duffels in between sips of the vodka. He hadn't spent enough time at the ranch lately anyway. His mother, at least, would be happy with the unexpected visit which would bring him close to his family home.

At the knock on the door, he called, "Coming." He tossed back the last of the vodka, zipped the duffels and walked over to the door.

"They're on the bed," he said as he swung it open, then stopped.

Zoe Smythe stood on the other side.

7

Behind her back, Zoe thumbed her bare left ring finger. Then she dropped her hands and lifted her chin, a movement that belied her stuttering heartbeat. She hoped she looked more confident than she felt.

Colin towered over her, dressed in black slacks and a crisp white shirt that set off his sun-bronzed skin. A wine-colored tie complemented his bottle-green eyes that were wide with surprise. But his expression quickly turned to appreciation as he raked his gaze over her. She hadn't been sure what to wear for a tryst, but from his reaction, she assumed the simple red wrap dress would suffice—at least until he removed it.

Emboldened, she conjured up a smile. "You were saying that something's on the bed?"

"Us," he said hoarsely, taking her hand and pulling her inside. Without breaking eye contact, he put the Privacy sign on the knob and closed the door. The kiss he lowered onto her mouth was fierce and left her breathless. He led her to the edge of the bed—not the log-hewn model she'd pictured for him when she'd first met him on the plane and he'd made the comment about getting home to sleep in his bed, but aptly masculine in wrought iron and as massive as she imagined. He paused long enough to shove two duffel bags to the floor.

"You're leaving?" she asked, suddenly anxious.

"Not anymore," he said, lying back and pulling her on top of his big body. "I didn't think you'd come." He ran his hands down her spine and over her buttocks, pulling her sex against his burgeoning erection.

Despite the delicious sensations flooding her womb, panic seized her. "So you weren't serious about…me knocking on your door?"

He rolled her over and kissed her hard, slanting his mouth over hers possessively. When he lifted his head, he stared into her eyes. "I was very serious, but I felt bad about pressuring you. I was going to leave so you didn't have to worry about seeing me again."

"I'm not here because you pressured me," she said, her chest rising and falling with rapid breaths.

"Why *are* you here?"

He seemed so focused on her answer that she chose her words carefully. It was important they both understand the limits of what they were about to do. "I want to experience something exciting," she whispered, "before I walk down the aisle." She picked up the end of his tie. "I have fantasies…."

In the dim lighting of the room, his eyes smoldered. "So do I."

Her heart thudded in anticipation. "So we understand each other?"

"A week of fun and games before you leave the country."

"No guilt and no strings," she murmured. "Just sex."

"I think I'm up to the job," he said with a heart-stopping grin. "Any special requests?"

How had she put it in her letter? She hesitated, then decided they were way past being coy with each other. "Tie me up, Colin. And make love to me six different ways."

His breath came out in a low groan as his cock surged against her thigh. "Yes, ma'am." Then a serious expression crossed his handsome face. "We should establish some safe words."

"Safe words?"

He smoothed the hair back from her face with his thumb. "Words to indicate whether we feel uncomfortable with anything the other person is doing. I want you to feel completely secure."

She nodded, grateful that he cared. "For example?"

He shrugged. "I've never done this before, but how about the universal *green, yellow,* and *red?*"

"*Green* means to keep going?" she asked.

"Right. *Yellow* means to slow down, and *red* means to stop. Does that work for you?"

She nodded, her trust in him blossoming.

"Any other ground rules?" he asked.

"No pictures," she said.

"Of course not."

"We also use a condom."

"Absolutely."

"No permanent…abrasions." She didn't want to have to use body makeup for her wedding.

He shook his head. "Don't worry."

"No questions about our personal lives."

He pursed his mouth, then nodded. "Okay."

"And no…guests."

His thick blond eyebrows rose. "Trust me, Zoe, I wasn't planning on sharing you."

"Good," she said, exhaling in relief and pleasure.

"Good." Then he winked. "We'll go shopping tomorrow for some things to make this a little more…interesting."

A thrill barbed through her at the promise of a sexual adventure.

"Meanwhile," he said, lowering his head, "we'll have to improvise." He bit lightly on her nipple through her clothes.

Zoe moaned and undulated against him, feeling languid and expansive in her decision to submit to his ministrations. Her pulse synched to the tribal throb of the music playing overhead. Her head spun as if she were drunk.

Colin tugged at the ribbon that held her dress closed at the waist and allowed the fabric to fall open. He sucked in a breath at the sight of her red bra and panties. "You look good enough to eat."

"I hope so," she crooned, feeling like a different woman. This entire conversation seemed surreal—these weren't words that normally came out of her mouth.

He nuzzled her neck, then eased the dress off her shoulders. As he kissed a path along the edge of her bra, she pushed her hands into his hair and urged his mouth to her breasts. Instead he rose above her, then unknotted and removed his tie. At the masterful look in his eye, her heart rate accelerated.

He caught her wrists above her head with one hand and wound the tie around her wrists, crisscrossing the strip of silk in between. Zoe offered no resistance. When he secured the other end of the tie to a rail on the headboard of the bed, a wave of anticipation crashed over her. It was as if she were allowing him entrance to a secret passageway to her psyche. She tested the bindings, gratified but a little nervous to see that her hands were immobilized above her, leaving her arched and breathing hard under his gaze.

"How does it feel?" he asked.

"G-green," she whispered, extending her legs to stretch as long as she could on the bed.

He nodded approval, then knelt over her. Using his teeth, he nudged aside the fabric of her bra to allow her breasts to spill over the top. He licked and kissed her jutting nipples, sending shivers of delight coursing through her. Then he twisted the hardened peaks, sending sparkles of pleasure-pain through her body.

"What color?" he murmured.

"Green," she gasped, looking up at him through a haze of bliss.

He leaned over her and took a nipple between his teeth, then clamped down until she flinched. He eased the pressure, then bit down on the other one until Zoe grunted.

"What color?"

"Yellow," she said, panting. She had to pace herself.

He lowered his mouth to her again, but his time he laved her stinging nipples with his warm tongue, bathing them with soothing moisture and gentle caresses. She sighed at the excruciating delight.

Then he moved lower, kissing his way down her body, over her stomach and clamped his mouth over her sex through her panties.

Zoe sucked in a sharp breath, straining to look down at him. He blew his hot breath through the thin fabric barrier, igniting a blaze deep within her. Slowly, inch by inch, he slid the panties down her hips and thighs, lifting her to remove them. He stood and walked out of sight. A click sounded, then the bed was bathed in a low, golden light.

"Nice," he said, his gaze heavy as he took in her nakedness.

Remembering her Brazilian bikini wax, which left a tiny strip of dark hair on her mons but rendered her smooth elsewhere, Zoe tucked her knees together, suddenly shy.

"Oh, no," he growled, reaching for her knees. "I want in there. I want to see you and taste you."

"Take off your clothes," she murmured.

"Not yet." He pried her knees apart and air hit her

in places where she was bare…and wet. She could feel her own moisture on her thighs. Colin leaned forward and dipped his tongue into her folds. Zoe gasped and pulled against her restraints. Not having the use of her hands made her more focused on what he was doing to her and all the sensations—the new sleekness of her sex, the nubby texture of the natural cotton bedspread at her back, the brush of Colin's thick hair against her thighs as he devoured her.

She closed her eyes and moaned, feeling as if she were underwater. He lifted her knees over his shoulders and speared his tongue deep inside her. She writhed as the orgasm sliding around inside her began to build momentum. He worked the pebble of her desire with the tip of his tongue until she bucked from the mushrooming rapture. Her muscles tensed as the waves of ecstasy broke over her. Zoe thrashed against the bed and cried out, pulling at her bindings, a sting that doubled her pleasure.

Colin eased her hips down and fumbled furiously with his pants. She heard the slide of his zipper and the rip of a condom package, the snap of him sheathing himself. Then he lifted her ankles to his shoulders and with one thrust, entered her. The shock of his bigness filling her stole her breath.

She thought she might die from the pleasure.

COLIN THOUGHT HE MIGHT DIE from the pleasure. Zoe Smythe's body was so delectable, only the act of keeping his clothes on had kept him from erupting like a schoolboy. Now, sheathed in her honeyed center, her slippery folds caressing him like a glove, he felt himself losing control. The sight of her bound to his bed with his tie, her rosy, bitten nipples poking over the top of her red bra, her head thrown back in abandon, her dark hair fanned over the light-colored coverlet…it was too much.

He stopped, trying to delay his imminent release, holding on to her ankles for dear life, trying to gather himself. But being motionless only heightened the sense of her contracting around him, milking him. With a guttural noise, he gave in to the climax, contracting his hips and plunging into her as deep as physically possible. She drained him of every drop of his essence.

While Colin recovered, kissing her ankles and gently separating their bodies, he felt the first stirrings of trouble. He'd thought it would be fun to teach the curious American a thing or two about light bondage. Instead the experience had rocked his world.

He unbound her wrists, then rolled to lie next to her. Zoe turned her head and looked at him through a tangle of hair, her blue eyes passion-glazed and a smile playing on her mouth. In that moment he thought he'd never seen anything so damned beautiful. Panic flashed through his chest. He'd signed up for a week of this?

He got up from the bed on the pretext of finishing his drink. Pulling on his chin, he studied the impossibly sexy half-nude woman sprawled on his bed. Incredibly, his balls were already aching for her again. She pushed herself up, massaging her slender wrists where they'd been bound.

"Is everything okay?" she asked. "You haven't changed your mind, have you?"

Colin pursed his mouth. The lady wanted a week of wild sex to tide her over after she married some suburban mama's boy…and he intended to give her something to remember. He strode across his room and removed two tieback cords from the curtains, then turned back to Zoe and held them up. "Ready to take it up a notch?"

She angled her head, then smiled wide. "Green."

8

ZOE GLANCED AT COLIN ACROSS the store where they were shopping and, feeling impish, lifted a pair of handcuffs, her eyebrows raised in question.

He grinned, then nodded. She added the handcuffs to her basket that contained four Velcro straps, a blindfold and two lengths of lightweight chain, suitable for making necklaces or belts, or for something more…adventurous.

Colin made his way over to her and Zoe's stomach fluttered. He wore battered jeans, a thick navy turtleneck and scuffed brown boots. He hadn't shaved this morning, so his square jaw was dark with stubble, his blond hair wind-ruffled. He was quite possibly the most handsome man she'd ever seen. And the fact that he'd spent last night doing such erotic things to her was still hard to grasp. But her sore muscles and tender erogenous zones didn't lie. She had, in fact, spent the better part of the night tied to this man's bed.

Inside her purse, her cell phone rang. Her conscience twinged because it couldn't be anything other than America calling. She pulled it out and glanced at the screen. It was Kevin.

"Do you need to get that?" Colin asked.

"Yes," she murmured. By unspoken agreement, neither one of them had mentioned the people in their lives they were cheating on.

He took the basket from her. "I'll pay for these things. Come find me when you're ready."

Zoe nodded, feeling flushed. She walked toward the exit and connected the call. "Hello?"

But it was too late—her phone had already rolled over to voice mail. She could call him back, but avoiding him was preferable to talking to him and pretending that she was whiling away the days making final plans for the wedding. She paced the sidewalk, castigating herself for her behavior. How could she love Kevin and do what she was doing?

Because love and sex were two different things, she reasoned. Erica had said it best—it was too much to expect to have great sex *and* great love with one person. Maybe Dr. Alexander had been wrong. Maybe the two things *were* mutually exclusive. Maybe sex was good with someone you don't love because you don't have to worry about emotional fallout, because there's no future to the relationship. Take her and Colin, for example. If either one of them was looking for a relationship, the sex would immediately change because it would be in the context of everything else going on—their jobs, their extended family, their finances. Love trumped sex…love endured long after sex burned out.

The new-voice-mail indicator appeared on the screen. She listened to the message, worrying her lower lip.

"Hey, Zoe, it's me, Kev. Listen, I got a great opportunity to ride with some world-class cyclists who are in town training for the Tour de Georgia, so I'm going to Tybee Island for a week or so. I'll be back in Atlanta a couple of days after you get home. I probably won't have a lot of time to check e-mail or answer the phone, but I'll touch base when I can. Bye."

Zoe deleted the message, exhaling. Was it wrong to be glad that Kevin wasn't lonely and bored in Atlanta while she was having her sexual fantasies fulfilled in Sydney? As if that made the situation more justifiable.

She closed her eyes, waiting for the remorse to overwhelm her, to change her mind about the week ahead.

It didn't.

COLIN WATCHED ZOE FROM WHERE he stood paying for their provocative props. The call was from her fiancé, no doubt. She was struggling with her decision to submit to her desires with another man before she got married. It reinforced Colin's first impression of her—that at her core, Zoe Smythe was a loyal, good-hearted person. She had stepped out of herself when she'd joined him in the plane lavatory, and last night when she'd knocked on his door.

An irrational stab of jealousy barbed through him.

Who was this man who'd captured the beauty's heart? And did he really deserve her if he couldn't satisfy her physically?

"Colin?"

He turned at the sound of his name, chagrined to see Benjamin Rook heading his way, dressed in a suit, holding a cardboard cone of fish-and-chips for lunch. "Hi, Ben."

Ben looked puzzled. "I got your message last night. I thought you were going to Canberra."

"I was, mate," Colin said. "Change of plans."

Ben glanced at the items the clerk was ringing up. Colin winced inwardly at the motley collection—blindfold, handcuffs, straps and chains.

His friend's eyebrows climbed, then he punched Colin's arm. "I see Lauren is back in town."

"Uh, Ben—"

"Sorry about that," Zoe said, walking up to him, stashing her phone. When she looked up, she stopped and glanced back and forth between Colin and Ben, while Ben glanced between Colin and Zoe.

She must have felt the tension in the air because she blanched. "I'm sorry—I interrupted."

"It's okay," Colin said quickly, feeling his mate bristle. "Zoe Smythe, this is Benjamin Rook. Ben, this is Zoe."

"Hello," she ventured.

"Nice to meet you," Ben said crisply. "Are you visiting from America?"

Zoe nodded. "I'm from Atlanta."

Ben cut his gaze to Colin, then shifted. "Atlanta, huh?"

Colin pressed his lips together and paid the cashier, knowing his friend was thinking the worst of him—and rightly so.

"Ben is a colleague," Colin cut in.

"More like a minion," Ben corrected with a smile that belied the underlying sarcasm of his voice. "It's my job to keep Colin diverted. He has a short attention span."

Zoe returned a shaky smile. Colin set his jaw and glared at his friend.

"Well, I'll let you get back to your shopping," Ben said, nodding to the bag Colin took from the clerk, which clanked loudly.

"And you to your lunch," Colin returned evenly. "I'll get back to you about the meeting."

Ben gave him a curt nod, and Colin could only watch his friend walk away. The man stopped at the first trash can he came to and tossed his uneaten food into it with more vehemence than necessary. Colin acknowledged a pang of remorse. He hadn't meant for anyone to get hurt over this.

"Is everything okay?" Zoe asked. "I have a feeling that I intruded on a private conversation."

"No worries," he assured her. "Just a few…complications. How are things on the home front?"

"Fine. Just a few…complications."

He nodded. They both needed to tread lightly to keep from injuring innocent parties.

"Speaking of which," she said, gesturing to her purse, "I need to check my e-mail and take care of some things."

"Last-minute wedding details?" he asked mildly.

She hesitated, then nodded.

"And I should check in with my office," he said, raking his hand over his jaw. "Do you want me to drop you back at the resort?"

"Actually, I was wondering if you could point me in the direction of a jewelry store."

Was she having her engagement ring sized? Appraised? Buying something for her groom? "The area next to the Circular Quay is called The Rocks—you'll find lots of jewelry stores there."

"Okay, thanks." She smiled and pointed. "That's this way, right?"

"Yeah, a couple hundred meters. Shall I walk with you?"

"No, I'm fine," she said, backing up. She seemed eager to get away from him. The phone call and Benjamin's reaction must have spooked her. It spooked him, too, because considering the lines they were crossing, why wasn't he calling off their arrangement? And why wasn't she?

Because, he realized as their hungry gazes locked, despite the risks, both of them were impatiently looking forward to trying out the props in the bag he had tucked underneath his arm. Unbidden, his cock jumped.

"Room service, my place, seven o'clock?" he ventured.

A wicked smile curved her mouth and she nodded. Colin's heart thudded in his chest and his vision tunneled until only the two of them were standing on the sidewalk, regardless of the noisy traffic and pedestrians rushing past. It was bizarre how in tune their bodies were to one another…as if they had been acquainted for years. Colin had never given much thought to the supernatural, but the instantaneous and powerful attraction he felt for this American seemed almost otherworldly. Maybe they'd known each other in another time….

Zoe turned and walked away from him. Colin watched the swing of her curvy behind for a few seconds, then shook the foolishness from his head. He was thinking with the wrong head, trying to pin something special on this illicit pact they'd made. But it was just sex, he told himself as he walked in the opposite direction. Nothing to get his heart in a bind over….

ZOE WALKED AWAY FROM COLIN, trying not to read anything into how let down she felt leaving him. But after waking up together, showering, having breakfast in his room and going on their little shopping expedition, they needed a break from each other. And that man Benjamin—Colin was clearly uncomfortable having the man see him with her.

She walked to The Rocks, glad that Colin had reminded her of the eclectic area with some of the oldest architecture in Sydney. The buildings were filled with art galleries, dress shops, shoe stores, bookstores, delis, bakeries, coffee shops and jewelry stores. Zoe whiled away the afternoon wandering in and out of the storefronts, delighted to find a jewelry maker working on a sterling silver locket in her studio. When she noticed Zoe's interest, she smiled.

"Do you make jewelry yourself?"

Zoe nodded, feeling shy. "Nothing intricate, just a few pieces for myself and for friends."

"That's how we all start," the woman said. "Do you work in metals?"

"Sterling links, although I don't make my own."

"And stones?"

"Semiprecious." Zoe wet her lips, hesitant to ask a jeweler about her sources. "Actually, I've been looking for loose opals to add to bracelets I'm making. Do you know of any places around here where I can buy them?"

"Uncut?"

"Cut but unpolished," Zoe said, thinking that she would be pressed for time when she returned to Atlanta to finish the bracelets.

The woman stopped to think. "There are a couple of jewelers in Manly who sometimes deal in unpolished stones. Otherwise, you'd probably need to shop closer to the mines at Lightning Ridge. Are you visiting?"

Zoe nodded.

"You might have better luck ordering them online and having them shipped to you," the woman said.

Zoe thanked her, then bought a pair of stunning earrings from the woman and moved on. She stopped for an iced coffee, then found a bench in a sunny spot to check her e-mail. Four more messages from her mother about changes to the reception dinner seating chart:

James Aldrich was sitting alone, but now wants to bring his new boyfriend (yes, boyfriend, he chose your wedding reception to come out of the closet).

The Donnellys just found out that the Feltons are coming and would like to sit at the same table.

Allison Armus wants to know if she can bring her own food—she's on a special diet.

Marisa Sun RSVP'd to bring her man friend, but would now like to bring her shih tzu, Moppet.

Zoe winced at the onset of an instant headache and saved the e-mails to reference later. When she saw Erica's name in her in-box, she clicked on the note, happy for a diversion.

Arrived home safely. Jim was happy to see me. Hope you're having a good time. Did you happen to run into the Aussie from first class again? ☺

Zoe gasped. Had Erica noticed something between her and Colin, or was she just teasing? Zoe wrote a quick note back hoping to nip her friend's taunts in the bud.

Glad your trip was safe and that Jim missed you. Am having a good time. Regarding Aussie from first class: Ha, ha. I'll call you when I get back home.

Chewing on her thumbnail, Zoe hit the reply button. Then she succumbed to temptation and pulled up an Internet search window. She typed in *Colin Cannon Sydney* and hit Enter. While she waited for the search results, she looked over her shoulder, half afraid that Colin would catch her spying on him. When the results page loaded, her eyes widened. There were several mentions of Colin in the local newspapers. He was a former professional soccer player, and after retiring, he'd taken over managing his own invest- ments, which included commercial property all over New South Wales. He was worth millions. Zoe swal- lowed hard and clicked on the image results.

There was a picture of Colin in his soccer uniform, with his team. His hair was longer and his body was ripped, but smaller, not yet matured into his frame. Subsequent photos featured him with women—a lot of women. Beautiful women, all shapes and sizes. Apparently he was known around town as a con- firmed bachelor and a bit of a playboy. She glanced at the title of a recent picture of him with a stunning, busty blonde with doe eyes. *Colin Cannon and Lauren Rook leave a fund-raising dinner.*

Zoe frowned as a memory stirred. *Rook*—the man Colin had been talking to today, the man he'd be- grudgingly introduced her to, had also been named

Rook. That couldn't be a coincidence, probably brother and sister. In hindsight, from Benjamin's comments and body language, he probably assumed that something was going on between them, that Colin was cheating on his sister. No wonder Colin had left. He was probably performing damage control, either convincing Benjamin not to tell his sister…or maybe coming clean with his girlfriend.

Her mind went to the black velvet ring box that had fallen out of his jacket pocket on the plane—it was obviously meant for Lauren Rook. Did Benjamin know that Colin was on the verge of proposing?

Zoe closed the pages, wishing she hadn't given in to her curiosity. It was clear that this little layover fling might affect more than just the two of them. Worse, she felt herself being drawn deeper into this man.

She sat on the bench for a long time, trying to decide whether to make the seven o'clock rendezvous.

Red…yellow…or green?

9

COLIN CHECKED HIS WATCH—twenty minutes past seven. He paced, worried that after the call from her fiancé, and after having the afternoon to think about what they were doing, Zoe had changed her mind about indulging in her sexual fantasies with him.

But what bothered him as much as the possibility that she'd changed her mind was the fact that it left him at loose ends. He had spent the afternoon trying to catch up on paperwork, but had been distracted and restless throughout.

He'd tried to call Benjamin, but his friend wasn't answering his phone—at least not for Colin. Which was just as well considering he wouldn't know what to say anyway. He hadn't planned for this fling to happen, hadn't planned to do something to hurt Lauren, but this thing with Zoe was like a locomotive—he couldn't seem to stop it.

Colin checked his watch again, then cursed and poured himself a drink. Since when had a woman kept him pent-up like a teenager? He picked up the remote control and turned up the music on the stereo—sultry American rhythm and blues for his sultry American.

A knock sounded and he exhaled in relief, feeling perilously like an addict about to get his fix. When he opened the door, Zoe stood there dressed in a sleeveless little black dress, her eye makeup dark and dramatic, her hair pulled back from her face severely. A black choker encircled her neck. She looked sexy as hell.

"Sorry I'm late," she murmured.

"No worries," he said, stepping aside to allow her to enter. The dress hugged her slender curves, stopping well above the knee. His hands fairly shook from wanting to tear it off. "Would you like a drink?"

She hesitated, then wet her lips. "Martini, extra dirty?"

Colin swallowed hard. "Coming up."

While he made the drink, he watched her walk around his room, taking in the view of the city at dusk. She moved with effortless grace, a gentle elegance that gave no hint of her darker inclinations. The paradox fascinated him.

"I think I bought this resort because of the view from these windows," he said. "I never get tired of looking at it."

"So you live here full-time?" she asked.

It was as close to a personal question as she'd asked. He nodded. "I had a home in the city, but this is closer to the office and since I wound up staying here most of the time, I moved in." He walked over to hand her the drink.

"It's lovely," she said.

Colin lifted his glass to clink hers. "So are you."

She smiled and drank deeply—for courage? Or like him, simply to take the edge off her raw emotions? He wanted to know what was going on in her head, but he knew the danger in becoming too close.

Both of them did.

"Are you hungry for dinner?" he asked instead.

"Maybe afterward," she said, then her eyes went smoky over the rim of her glass.

Lust surged through Colin's body. He had told himself tonight they would have a nice dinner, take it slow. But her blatant desire for him made him want to toss her on the bed and gorge on her body. Dinner forgotten, he set his jaw to rein in his libido. "Dance for me."

She took another deep drink from her glass, then set it down. Closing her eyes, she began to sway back and forth with the music, moving her shoulders and her hips, as she had the night he'd watched her at the music festival. He'd itched to touch her then, but had managed to walk away. Tonight, however, he planned to touch every square inch of her incredible body.

She lifted her arms over her head and turned in a slow circle to the bass of the music. His cock began to throb in time with her movements and the acoustics in the room. Zoe danced like she made love— with sure, deft motions and innate rhythm. His longing for her grew with every swing of her hips, as did his erection. He enjoyed her sensual dance until the song ended and she opened her blue eyes, glazed with passion.

"Take off your dress," he said.

After a heartbeat's hesitation, she reached behind her to lower a zipper with agonizing slowness. Then she slid the black dress off her shoulders, revealing the tiny ribbon straps of a black bra, then the lacy cups that barely restrained her generous breasts. Colin groaned and tossed back the rest of his drink. She shimmied the dress lower, past a narrow waist and flaring hips, then stepped out of it to stand before him in a scrap of black lace that barely covered her secrets, the overtaxed bra, the black choker and a pair of black stiletto heels.

He would've shot his load on the spot if not for the fact that he'd be denied the unbearable pleasure of burying himself in her body.

"Take down your hair," he ordered.

With the flip of her hand and a toss of her head, her dark hair fell over her shoulders in cascading waves. He swallowed, longing to drive his hands into it. Colin leaned over and from a drawer in a table next to his bed, he removed the black satin blindfold and the Velcro straps they had purchased.

"Come to me," he said, his voice gravelly.

She walked to the bed with a glitter of anticipation in her eyes. Her cheeks were pink, her lips softened.

"Turn around," he said, then stood behind her and secured the blindfold over her eyes, tying it in back. He buried his face in her fragrant, silken hair, then reached around and cupped her full breasts, teasing the tips through the thin fabric of her bra. When she pushed back against him, though, he pulled away, determined to make the night last as long as possible. He was already so worked up for her that her body against his would be the end.

Colin turned up the music, then drank in the sight of her. She stood still, moving her head, trying to detect where he was in the room. After another minute of watching her, he retrieved her martini, walked to her and wrapped her fingers around the cold stem of the glass. While she sipped the drink, he fastened the Velcro straps to the four posts of his bed, his balls aching at the implication of the sensual task. The telltale noise of separating the two sides of the straps left no question as to what he was doing.

"How are you feeling?" he asked, mindful of the possibility that he might push things too far or that she would change her mind midstream.

"Green," she said, turning her head in his direction. As if to punctuate, she used her teeth to remove the two olives from the tiny skewer and chewed them slowly.

Colin took the empty glass from her hand and set it on some flat surface—his body was so hard from wanting her, he could barely process rational thought. He leaned over and curved his hand around the nape of her neck, holding her still for a thorough kiss, then easing her down and back on the coverlet. When he withdrew, she whimpered, but he put his finger to her lips. "Take off your bra."

She reached around with both hands to unfasten her bra, freeing her amazing breasts. The dark pink tips were puffy and distended.

Colin's throat convulsed. "Now your panties."

"They're…expendable," she murmured.

His cock surged. Obliging, he leaned down and ran his finger inside the edges of the minuscule black underwear, finding silky skin and eliciting a soft moan from her before moving to the flimsy side straps and ripping them loose. He removed the destroyed underwear and tossed it aside. Zoe was lying on his bed naked except for the choker, the blindfold and the stilettos.

If he died now, Colin decided, he'd have a smile on his face.

He lifted one of her hands and turned it over, kissing her slender wrist before encircling it with a Velcro strap and pulling up the slack, effectively securing her to the bedpost.

"How are you doing?" he asked, his voice hoarse with need.

"Green," she whispered.

He knelt over her, then kissed the other palm and secured her second arm to the other bedpost.

"How about now?" he asked.

"Green."

He lifted her foot and swirled his tongue around

her ankle bone as he slipped off her shoe and let it drop to the floor. She stiffened, then sighed, offering no resistance as he closed the free end of one of the Velcro straps around her ankle, binding her to a third bedpost.

"Now?" he asked.

"Green," she said breathlessly.

Gratified, he removed her other shoe, and kissed the ankle before securing it to the last bedpost. She lay spread-eagled, her breasts thrust in the air and her femininity open to his appraisal. His mouth watered and his mind reeled at the sight of her. Even more moving, though, was the knowledge that she trusted him with her safety, and with her pleasure.

"Now?" he asked, holding his breath.

"Green, green, green," she said, her voice ending on a moan.

It was all the encouragement he needed. Colin stripped out of his clothes as quickly as he could. He would never compromise Zoe's trust by taking a photo of her, but he stared at her long and hard, knowing he'd never forget the picture she made, lying on his bed, waiting for him to take her to places she'd never been.

ZOE TESTED THE RESTRAINTS pulling her in four directions by drawing in slightly. The Velcro straps around her wrists and ankles were gentle against her skin, but held her firmly. She couldn't move more than a few inches in any direction.

Her heart raced at the knowledge that she was totally at the mercy of the physical, sensual man who had bound her to his bed. The blindfold entirely obscured her vision and blocked the light. She yearned to see him, but acknowledged that not being able to anticipate his actions ratcheted her adrenaline even higher.

From the swish of clothing and the slide of a zipper, she knew he was undressing that big, magnificent body of his. She could feel his hungry gaze on her all the while, like a breeze, sweeping over her hardened nipples, and the newly waxed, sensitized skin around her sex. With her arms and legs spread wide, nothing was hidden from him, leaving her feeling utterly vulnerable…and aroused.

Without the benefit of her sight, her other senses became more acute, zoning in on the slide of her hair against the coverlet as she moved her head back and forth, the pulsating beat of the moody music floating from the ceiling, the taste of salty olives lingering on her lips, the musky scent of her intimate nest teasing her nostrils.

When the mattress dipped with his weight, the restraints tightened, reminding her of her bondage. She tensed, unsure of what he would do first, on which part of her body he would unleash his sensual assault.

He chose her lips. He kissed her hard, crushing his mouth against hers, although it was the only place their bodies touched. When he lifted his mouth, she strained upward to follow him, but was hindered by her restraints.

Next he kissed her arms, moving from her captured wrists to the insides of her elbows, nuzzling the delicate skin. His body hovered over hers, the coarse hair on his chest tickling her breasts, his rigid shaft jabbing into her stomach. Pinpoints of pleasure lit up her entire body. She writhed beneath him, craving full body contact.

Instead he nibbled his way down her body, sinking his teeth into her neck, her collarbone, her shoulder, increasing pressure as he moved into more fleshy areas. She moaned her approval, arching into him. After much delicious torment, he clasped one turgid nipple between his teeth and bit down.

Zoe flinched as pleasure-pain zinged through her torso. A whimpering sound escaped from her. He moved to the other nipple and she tensed, this time ready for the satisfying sting when it came.

"How are you feeling?" he murmured against her skin.

"Green," she whispered.

He kneaded her breasts with his big hands, applying more and more pressure. Her thighs were wet and cool from the moisture pooling there. She rolled her shoulders, reveling in the fact that he was so attentive to her breasts, her most sensitive erogenous zones. Kevin never—

Zoe went still. Where had that thought come from?

"Are you okay?" Colin said thickly.

She chastised herself for allowing the rogue thought to materialize. She'd be fine if she simply focused on the pleasure coursing through her body. Forcing everything else from her mind, she said, "Yes. I mean…green."

He resumed his ministrations, pulling on her nipples, harder and faster, until they felt long and swollen. She bit into her lip and shuddered with each twinge of luxurious pain. Her nerve endings were going wild, sending sensations to disconnected parts of her body. Vibrations shook her womb. She thrashed her head from side to side and pulled against the wrist restraints. The leverage amplified the shards of pleasure spinning through her. He kept up the pressure and the rhythm until she gritted her teeth and murmured, "Yellow."

Instantly he slowed and his movements gentled. He pulled the tender tips into his mouth for a soothing bath, murmuring reassurances. Zoe relaxed her muscles and released a long, cleansing sigh. She wriggled her fingers and toes to fend off the stinging sensations of compromised circulation. As he continued to nuzzle her breasts, he lowered his hand to the juncture of her thighs and without warning, inserted one large finger into her slick channel.

She groaned and her hips contracted at the force and the fullness. He made love to her with his hand and after several long strokes, inserted two fingers.

"How are you doing?" he rasped.

"Green," she said, then gasped when he inserted a third finger.

"Now?"

"G-green," she managed, but her knees jerked, testing the ankle restraints. Zoe mewled at the fierceness of his thrusting fingers…and the precision. Colin was hitting her G-spot, and a spot for every other letter of the alphabet. An orgasm hit her like a storm, more sudden and deep-seated than anything she'd ever experienced. She cried out his name and bucked, contracting around his strong hand, riding the long, crashing waves of pleasure so intense, it left her lightheaded.

When her spasms finally ceased, Colin removed his hand. "Are you okay?" he murmured.

She nodded against the bed. "Yes."

"Do you want me to release you?"

She hesitated, flexing her hands and feet to test her circulation. Then she lifted her head and smiled in his direction, wishing she could see him. "Only if you're finished."

In response, he left the bed. For a few seconds, Zoe panicked, thinking she'd said something wrong. Then she heard the sound of a condom package being ripped open. And then she was being engulfed by his big warm body. He kissed her, exploring her mouth with his tongue while the tip of his cock teased her clit. Zoe moaned into his mouth, and kicked at the ankle restraints in frustration.

Colin broke the kiss. "Is this what you want?" He

moved his hips a fraction, inserting the knob of his stiff shaft into her.

Zoe moaned and clenched around him. "Yes… please…now."

With a guttural noise, he buried himself inside her, filling her completely. Zoe gasped, longing to wrap her arms around him, to feel the muscles in his back. But with his weight on top of her, the restraints pulled tighter, applying more pressure, the tension just short of pain. Colin pumped into her like a machine, dropping hard kisses and bites on her collarbone, the hair on his chest teasing her sensitized nipples.

The onslaught to her senses began to coax another climax from her belly. She clenched around him, meeting him thrust for thrust as the tremors in her midsection began to consume her. From his ragged breathing, she knew he was also nearing the end, and the knowledge spurred her passion even higher.

She climaxed with a full-body contraction, wrenching against the straps that pulled her in all directions, tightening around him like a spring. "Oh, Colin…Colin…yes…*yesss.*"

With one powerful thrust, his body shuddered like an earthquake between her thighs. He bellowed his satisfaction against her neck and pulsed inside her for long minutes as their hearts thumped against each other. Cloaked in darkness, Zoe was disoriented. For a while she felt as if she were floating, suspended in air. Then she felt the coverlet at her back, the bindings on her limbs, and her equilibrium slowly returned. Once their bodies had quieted, he withdrew, still breathing hard, and removed her blindfold.

Zoe blinked into the sudden light, shocked and excited by the image of her bound body, his nudity covering hers. The intensity in Colin's hooded green eyes gave her pause, but it was the flutter of her heart that planted a seed of worry in her mind.

In the middle of their lovemaking, she had unconsciously compared Colin's techniques to Kevin's, and found Kevin wanting. And now this strange sense of exhilaration came over her when she looked at Colin. Was she starting to have feelings for this man?

Then, thankfully, his gaze turned teasing. "For a moment there, I thought I might have a heart attack." He pushed himself up and discarded the rubber, then quickly freed her wrists and ankles. From a nearby closet, he removed two white spa robes and extended one to her before shrugging into one himself.

Zoe sat up, determined to keep the mood light. "And what would I have done?" She pulled on the robe, rubbing a reddened wrist.

He retrieved a jar of lotion from the nightstand, unscrewed the lid and dipped his fingers inside. "You would've had to gnaw your way to freedom," he said, his eyes twinkling. Then he picked up her arm to massage the cool white lotion into the skin where the straps had left marks.

Zoe stared at his hands, so large and strong, yet

so gentle. Neither one of them spoke while he moved to the other wrist, then administered to both ankles. Her heart swerved crazily in her chest. It was the most intimate moment she'd ever shared with a man. "Thank you," she whispered.

"You're welcome," he said, and for a split second, that intensity was back in his eyes. He flashed that disarming smile. "I'm ready for some nourishment. How about you?"

She nodded enthusiastically, hoping this strange feeling in her stomach was simply hunger.

After they ordered room service, Colin poured them both another drink and made small talk. Zoe kept waiting for awkwardness to descend, but he was at ease and confident and she was happy to follow his lead. It made her feel very adult, that she could indulge in her sexual fantasies with a man who took it in stride, without labeling her as strange or lascivious. And without making her feel the least bit threatened.

"So...what are your plans for tomorrow?" he asked lightly.

Zoe shrugged. "Nothing definite, but I'd like to visit Manly Beach before I leave, so I might take the ferry over."

Colin handed her another "extra dirty" martini, thick with olive juice and studded with olives. "I have a better idea. I'll take you to Manly on my boat."

"That's not necessary—" she protested.

"We'll make a day of it," he cut in congenially. "It'll be great fun."

It would be fun, she conceded. But spending the day on a boat with Colin in the open air and sea seemed too much like a date, and their arrangement was supposed to be strictly about sex.

"A boat has lots of ropes," he added with a wicked smile.

Zoe's mouth curved in relief that he, too, was mindful of their agreement. And she'd be lying if she said she wasn't titillated by the prospect of being bound to this man's mast. "What time do we set sail?"

10

Zoe had never seen so much rope in her life—white rope, striped rope, nylon rope, cotton rope, thin rope, thick rope. Rope tied to cleats, rope tied to sails, rope tied to the dock and rope simply lying on the floor of the boat tied in neat bundles.

Colin grinned up at her where she stood on the dock. "For the record, on a boat, rope is referred to as *line*."

Zoe's midsection tightened—her body responded to him as if a bell had sounded. Considering their lovemaking session the night before, she marveled that she could be aroused so quickly, but so far, no matter how sated she was, she still wanted him. Even accepting his strong hand to steady her as she stepped down into the sparkling white sailboat gave her a thrill.

From the desire that smoldered in his eyes, Colin was also affected by their nearness. "Later I'll show you how to tie a few knots," he murmured, his voice teasing.

"I'll take you up on that, Captain."

His laughter carried over the breeze blowing. She

wished she could have taken a picture of him at that moment, smiling wide, his eyes bright, his blond hair wind-ruffled. He was so handsome, he made the breath hitch in her lungs. Dressed in blue swim trunks and T-shirt, he looked every inch the athlete that he'd been most of his life. Her mouth watered to ask him about his past, but she'd been the one who'd insisted that they not ask each other personal questions. Instead she swept an approving glance over the boat named *Horizon Bound.* "How big is it?"

"*She* is about ten meters long," he said cheerfully. "Boats are female, you know, to keep a lonely sailor company when he's out on the water." He pointed up. "Her sail is about three meters. Big enough to be a comfortable ride, but small enough for one man to handle alone. And there's the outboard motor if the wind fails me."

So he often went out on his boat alone? As soon as the question materialized, Zoe chided herself—it wasn't any of her business. And maybe he manned the boat alone even when he had company. Or, considering his wealth, he probably had a larger boat for entertaining.

"Do you swim?" he asked.

"Yes."

"How well?"

"I've had lifesaving training."

"Excellent. Maybe we can stop and take a dip along the way. You did wear your cossie, didn't you?"

She squinted. "Excuse me?"

"Bathing suit," he clarified, grinning. "No worries if you didn't. We'll just find somewhere private."

"I'm wearing it," she said with a laugh. "But I was hoping to actually *make* it to Manly Beach."

He pouted, then nodded toward a small open door. "You can take your bag belowdeck and look around if you like. There's a head if you need to use it."

Zoe carefully descended the narrow steps to the cabin. To her left was a small bathroom—the head. To her right was a bench seat and a foldaway table. Past the bathroom was a tiny kitchen with a sink and miniature appliances. Straight ahead through another door was a bed that ran wall to wall—big enough to sleep two, she couldn't help noticing. It was close quarters, especially for a man of Colin's size, but more than adequate for a day's outing. And it was another glimpse into Colin's lifestyle, one totally foreign to her.

From her bag, her cell phone pinged, indicating she had e-mail. Zoe sighed and pulled out the phone, glancing at the subject lines as the notes downloaded. Three more messages from her mother, two concerning changes to the reception dinner seating chart, and one about the florist.

Zoe put a hand to her temple as the incongruity of the situation hit her. What was she doing? Playing out her fantasies with a virtual stranger while on the other side of the world, her mother and a team of specialists worked to create the perfect wedding for her and her fiancé. She glanced down at her bare finger where a white tan line betrayed her. She had thought by taking off the ring, she could forget about her commitment.

And the worst part? She had.

But simply putting something out of your mind didn't make it disappear. It was there, waiting for her. Hanging back until her fantasy week had run its course.

"Will you grab us a couple of brews from the re-frigerator?" Colin called down, breaking into her troubled thoughts.

Happy for the diversion, she called, "Sure."

Zoe turned off the phone and pushed it to the bottom of her bag. After pulling two beers from the fridge, she climbed up the stairs to rejoin him on the deck. "Nice living quarters."

He was unwinding a rope from a cleat on the dock. "Glad you like it."

Zoe stuck the beers in cup holders next to the captain's chair. "What can I do?"

He looked impressed that she'd offered, then pointed to the rear of the boat. "Untie that aft line and we'll shove off."

She moved to the back of the boat and unwound the line, looping the length like she'd seen him do, between thumb and elbow in large, neat circles to keep it from tangling.

"Very good," he said, nodding in approval. "You'll make a good first mate."

Frivolous praise, she knew, but the words evoked an unbidden image of them together…as a couple. She closed her eyes to banish the treacherous thought, telling herself to get a grip—this was all a fantasy. She'd be returning to reality—and Kevin—in a few short days.

"Everything okay?" he asked.

Zoe opened her eyes to find Colin studying her with concern.

"You're not seasick already, are you?"

"No," she assured him.

"Homesick?"

Guilt washed over her. She wasn't, but she should be. Embarrassed by her feelings, she couldn't bring herself to answer.

"No worries," he said with a wink. "We'll have fun today. Have a seat and a beer and we'll be on our way."

She took one of the bottles and settled into the rear bench seat, out of reach of the sail should it swing to the other side of the boat.

Colin used a long pole to push them away from the dock, relying on large buoys hanging over the side to ensure they didn't bump into adjacent boats as he maneuvered out of the slip.

She loved watching him move. Besides being so handsome, he was solid and well-proportioned, agile for a big man and in command of every muscle. No wonder he was such a good lover, she mused.

Kevin is an athlete, too, her mind whispered.

Zoe glanced up at the slack mainsail flapping in the wind and frowned at the symbolism.

She lifted her beer for a swallow and pulled her hat down to shield her eyes. She was starting to see things that weren't there...starting to read too much into small gestures...starting to listen to the voice in her head that asked *what if?*

There was no *what if,* she stubbornly reminded herself. There was only *going to be.*

When they were clear of the marina, Colin pulled the lines to tighten the mainsail. The stiff white fabric snapped, then caught the wind and the boat picked up speed.

"How far to Manly Beach?" she called.

"About eleven nautical kilometers—seven miles," he shouted back, securing the line holding the sail to a cleat on the side of the boat. "We could make it in about twenty minutes, but since it's such a fine day, I thought we'd take the scenic route, and stop by Manly for lunch."

She smiled her agreement, and inhaled the salt-scented air, her chest billowing with pleasure. It *was* a fine day—postcard perfect, the deep blue water broken by small whitecaps and jumping fish. It was breathtaking to look up the mainsail to the sky above. Cottony clouds looked close enough to touch. Gulls called out as they dipped and soared.

Colin reached into side storage compartments and pulled out two life jackets, placing them within reach.

Always cautious, she thought, recalling the system of safe words he'd suggested for their sex play. Would they reach *red* before the end of the week? A sensual shiver ran over her shoulders.

He grabbed the other beer and settled next to her, stretching out his long, muscular legs. Zoe acknowledged that her feeling of being off balance had little to do with the gentle rocking of the vessel as they skimmed along, following the twists and turns of the bay. They were sitting low in the boat, inches from the water. She couldn't resist leaning over the side and letting its coolness run through her fingers.

Zoe turned her head, taking in the enigmatic man next to her and their Technicolor surroundings. In a word, it was surreal.

"It doesn't get any better than this," he said, tilting his face up to the sun.

"You must spend a lot of time in America," Zoe remarked. "Sometimes your accent sounds diluted."

"That would be my mother's fault. She's American."

Zoe blinked in surprise. "She lives in the States?"

"No, she lives in Canberra, but after almost forty years, she still sounds like a Southern belle."

"She's from the South?"

"Born and raised in Atlanta," he said, affecting a southern drawl.

Zoe smiled. "Really?" Then she caught herself. "I'm sorry—we agreed no personal questions."

"It's fine," he said. "I don't mind talking about my family."

Zoe couldn't resist the invitation. "So your father is Australian?"

"Through and through."

"How did they meet?"

"He was a soccer player during university, and got the chance to tour in the States."

Like father, like son, she almost said before she remembered that she wasn't supposed to know anything about him.

"Back then Americans hadn't even heard of the game," he added. "He met my mother, and within a few days, somehow convinced her to marry him and move here."

Zoe smiled wistfully. "What a great story. Is your father still alive?"

"Oh, yeah. Stubborn old cuss. I don't know how Mom puts up with him."

"Do you have a big family?"

"Two younger brothers. They're both cattlemen."

"With families?"

"No, they're single, too."

He shifted on the seat and she realized she'd hit a nerve. Was he thinking about his own impending engagement?

"What's your family like?" he asked.

Zoe gave a little laugh. "Unfortunately, my parents don't have a love story."

His expression dimmed. "Divorced?"

"No, worse—they should have." She picked at the corner of the label on the beer bottle. "They're both good people, but they bring out the worst in each other."

"That's too bad," he murmured. "Do you have brothers and sisters?"

"No, it's just me."

"Caught in the middle, eh?"

She nodded. "The wedding—" At her gaffe, Zoe blanched. "I'm sorry…I shouldn't have mentioned it."

"It's okay," Colin said with a shrug. "It is what it is. You're getting married. I'm happy for you."

"You must think I'm a terrible person. I didn't come to Sydney with the intention of doing…this."

His expression turned philosophical as he sat forward, resting his elbows on his knees. "I don't think you're a terrible person. I take it your fiancé isn't adventurous between the sheets?"

She squirmed, reluctant to discuss her and Kevin's sex life. "We've…been together a long time."

"He doesn't know that you like to be restrained," he said matter-of-factly.

Her cheeks warmed. "He wouldn't understand. His mind doesn't go there."

He wagged his eyebrows and leaned closer. "But mine does."

Desire trumped guilt, stabbing her low and hard. "And mine," she whispered.

Colin drew on his bottle of beer, glancing all around them, then back to her, his eyes overcast with need. "How about we drop anchor and I give you that lesson on tying knots I promised you?"

Her body instantly began preparing itself—warming, moistening, expanding. Zoe brought her hand to her forehead in a mock salute and murmured, "Aye, aye, Captain."

11

THE DOUBLE HALF-HITCH knot across Zoe's bare stomach that he'd used to tie her up like a package was, Colin decided, a thing of beauty. The thick cotton cord was a perfect foil for her smooth, flawless skin. Her remarkable breasts poked through the system of cross ties, the tweaked nipples pert and red. Her dark hair fanned out behind her head. Her eyes were closed while a myriad of sensations played over her expressive, lovely face—pleasure, pain, joy, frustration. She was so hot he couldn't stand it.

He pumped into her body, reveling in the exquisite strength of her feminine walls surrounding his cock. As she contracted around his length and cried out in her second orgasm, Colin felt himself being pulled along. He gritted his teeth, trying to hold back, but he couldn't fight the tide of lust that raged through his body. He came forcefully, shooting a full load, his groans mingling with hers as he collapsed on top of her.

Colin exhaled and rolled to her side to keep from crushing her, then turned his head to look at her profile.

Zoe's eyes were still closed, her lips parted, her chest moving up and down as her breathing returned to normal. Satisfaction swelled in his chest that he was able to do this for her, to help her explore her deepest fantasies. But her heart obviously belonged to her fiancé. It was a shame because the man had no idea what a treasure he held.

"Is something wrong?" she asked.

He realized her eyes were open, that she'd caught him staring. "No. That was amazing, as always."

She smiled and nodded. "Are you going to untie me?"

He sighed. "I suppose I must before someone thinks the boat has been abandoned and boards to find out."

At the panicked look in her eyes, he laughed and began to free her bonds. As he loosened the knots, he kissed the tender areas of her skin where she had strained against the cords. "Who knew the knot-tying badge I earned in Scouts would come in so handy?"

She grinned. "You have Boy Scouts here?"

He nodded. "How many times have you visited my country?"

"Dozens. Although usually the layovers are just for a day or two, in Sydney, sometimes Melbourne. I was in Cairns twice and saw the Reef, but I haven't seen much of the rest of the country."

"How long have you been a flight attendant?"

She hesitated. Even though they'd talked about their families, he wondered if she would resist talking about herself.

"Since graduating college," she said finally. "I have a degree in communications and I speak a couple of other languages. I had planned to teach, but all I could think about was traveling…getting away."

From her parents? he wondered. "And have you seen the world?"

She nodded and pushed herself up, reaching for her clothes. "My language skills helped me secure a position as an international flight attendant. I've been lucky over the last ten years to see lots of exotic places and experience different cultures."

"You make it sound as if that's all coming to an end."

She was quiet while she put on her bikini top. Colin moved to fasten the tie behind her neck and she allowed him to help her, holding up her hair. He couldn't resist dropping a kiss on her silky shoulder. She sighed in response, then slid off the bed to finish dressing. "I'm giving up international flights so I can be home more."

"Ah. So you won't be coming back this way in the foreseeable future?"

"No," she said bluntly.

From a tiny shelf next to the bed his cell phone rang. Colin glanced at the screen and saw Benjamin's name. Remorse arrowed through him. "Sorry, I need to take this."

She picked up her tennis shoes and gave him a little smile. "I'll wait for you on deck, Captain."

He smiled at her attempt to lighten the mood—

both of them seemed a little preoccupied. As her shapely legs and feet disappeared up the steps, he connected the call he'd been dreading.

"Hi, Ben."

"Colin," Ben said, his voice curt. "I'm returning your calls."

"Ben, listen, mate…I don't know what to say. You know I care about Lauren, but—"

"But you need a girlfriend in Atlanta, too? And you bring her here for the month that Lauren is in New Zealand?"

Colin frowned. "What? No. I met Zoe on the flight back. She's only here for a few more days."

"So this isn't going anywhere?"

"No. In fact…she's getting married when she goes back to the States."

"Oh, that's rich."

"Come on, man, it just happened. She was looking to blow off some steam before her wedding, and Lauren has been pressuring me about getting engaged. We're just having a harmless little naughty."

Ben gave a rueful laugh. "Someday you're going to get your heart broken, and you deserve it, you skunk."

"So did you rat me out to your sister?"

"It's not my place," Ben said. "But I should warn you that she suspects something's up because you haven't answered her calls."

Colin massaged the bridge of his nose. "Thanks,

mate. So when can you and I get together again to talk about the Atlanta property?"

Silence vibrated over the line. "To be honest, I'm having second thoughts."

Colin scowled. "Because I haven't proposed to Lauren?"

"Blood is thicker than water, mate. I don't think it's a good idea to enter into a partnership with the bloke that my sister might wind up stabbing. It's not good for business or for family reunions."

"If I didn't know better, Ben, I'd think you were blackmailing me."

"Have fun with your American, Colin. When you get your donger out of a knot and you come to your senses, let me know."

Ben hung up. Colin disconnected the call and cursed at getting himself in such a bind. As he reached for his clothes, he stared at the lengths of cord lying on the bed that he'd used to wrap around every delicious inch of Zoe Smythe's body. And bloody hell, he started to get hard again.

Colin scrubbed his hand down his face. Ben was right—he was being a jerk toward Lauren. And Zoe was obviously having some misgivings about their arrangement. He rubbed at his breastbone. On top of everything else, he was starting to have these strange…*stirrings* when he was with Zoe.

This had to end.

He'd take her to Manly and they'd have fun for

the day. But sometime before they returned to the hotel, he'd find a way to call off their games. For everyone's sake.

ZOE STOOD LOOKING ACROSS the bay, watching other boats crisscross the blue waters—ferries taking tourists and commuters to Taronga Zoo, Rose Bay, Watsons Bay and Manly; commercial fishing water-craft rigged with poles and nets; and colorful cruise ships giving catered tours of the harbor.

One of the big cruisers motored by with its air horn blowing and well-dressed passengers waving. Her throat convulsed.

It was a wedding party.

The bride's white dress and veil shimmered in the sun; the tuxedoed groom was holding her hand high. They were dancing, celebrating the first day of the rest of their life together. The sheer joy on the bride's face mocked Zoe. She would bet *that* woman hadn't embarked on a kinky affair mere weeks before taking her vows.

She'd overheard Colin's raised voice on the phone, and suspected the conflict with the person on the other end had something to do with her.

Her body still pulsed from their lovemaking, her skin still bore the imprint of the cord that he'd used to restrict her movement while he did incredible things to her with his tongue…and other parts of his body. But afterward, when he'd asked about her career and her plans—the line of questioning had seemed too intimate.

Worse, she was starting to experience something when she looked at him, something that felt dangerously close to attachment, and that simply couldn't happen. The allure of the affair had always been sex with no strings. The fantasy with no emotional investment. Things were getting too sticky. It would be best to part as friends now and go back to their respective worlds before anyone else got hurt.

Zoe inhaled deeply, filled with resolve. They would have a fun afternoon in Manly, but sometime before they returned to the resort, she'd find a way to end their arrangement.

For everyone's sake.

At a noise behind her, she turned to see Colin emerge from the cabin. She was struck anew by his masculine good looks. He smiled, but she could tell it was forced.

"What's all the commotion out here?"

"A wedding party on a harbor cruise ship," she said, pointing.

"Ah." He nodded, then cleared his throat. "I guess I'd better get you to Manly before the day is gone."

"Sounds good," she said, returning a forced smile of her own.

He cranked up the anchor, tightened the mainsail and they were soon under way, a current of tension running between them. Zoe focused on the magnificent surroundings, the *swish, swish* of the water against the boat, the salty spray on her face and arms.

A few minutes later, Manly Wharf came into view. The bayside city reminded Zoe of Key West, with its mix of colonial architecture, trees and beaches. Except where the Keys had palm trees, Manly was known for the towering Norfolk Island pine trees along the harbor shore.

A dock employee came over to help guide the sailboat into an empty slip. Colin climbed out to secure the lines to dock cleats, then reached in to assist Zoe out of the boat. When he clasped her hand and pulled her up next to him, a jolt of awareness speared through her chest. His breath fanned over her cheek and her throat convulsed nervously.

A bizarre reaction considering all the intimacies they'd shared.

"Thanks," she murmured, pulling away and shouldering her bag.

Colin gave the man a tip, then they strolled toward the wharf. He suggested an outdoor café for lunch and she agreed, although neither of them exhibited much of an appetite. The activity around them filled in around their small talk. Although they both tried to put on a good face, Zoe was conscious of the anxiety vibrating between them.

At the end of their half-eaten meal, they strolled through the many shops and art galleries. Zoe knew Colin could probably afford anything he wanted, but when it came to shopping, he exhibited the same disinterest most men had, seemingly content to follow her in and out of shops. When they came to a jewelry store, Zoe decided to spare him.

"You don't have to go in. I'll just take a quick look around."

"I don't mind," he said with a congenial shrug.

They entered the shop and after glancing into several glass cases, Zoe asked the clerk if the store sold loose or unpolished opals. The woman looked regretful and shook her head.

"Do you know of a local resource?"

"Not in Manly, ma'am, I'm sorry." The woman squinted and leaned in closer. "What a beautiful necklace."

Zoe smiled and fingered the delicate wire-wrapped pendant she wore. "Thank you."

When Zoe turned, Colin was standing nearby wearing a grin. "Unpolished opals? Are you a smuggler?"

She laughed, then pressed her lips together, hesitant to respond. "I design jewelry as a hobby."

His eyebrows climbed. "Did you design the necklace that woman just commented on?"

Zoe nodded.

"And the choker you were wearing the night you came to my room?"

Her cheeks warmed. "Yes."

"Nice. Do you sell your designs in Atlanta?"

Zoe gave a little laugh. "No. I just make things for myself, and as gifts."

"And you need opals for something special?"

She bit into her lip. "I'm making bracelets for my bridesmaids and I thought opals would be a nice touch. It's no big deal, though. I can use another stone." She motioned toward the door. "Ready? I wouldn't mind a walk on the beach before we leave."

He was staring at her in the oddest way. Then he smiled and nodded, and she was relieved to see that some of the unspoken tension between them had dissipated. Maybe they could at least end on a good note.

The harbor foreshore was a generous curve of sand on a protected cove, extending into brilliantly colored waters of aqua, cobalt and indigo. Picturesque enough on its own, but framed by a row of gigantic Norfolk Island pines, it was a magical little slice of the world.

The afternoon temperatures had climbed, especially on the beach where the sun's rays were reflected. Colin removed his T-shirt and shoes, and Zoe followed suit. She tried not to stare at his powerful physique, but she couldn't help stealing a few glances under the brim of her hat. She acknowledged that even though she'd decided to end their arrangement, it would take a while for her body to become reconciled to the fact.

They strolled near the water's edge, at first maintaining an arm's length between them. But as they continued to walk in the frothy surf and soft sand, their bodies migrated closer and closer, like the opposite poles of magnets. Zoe's midsection began to hum a familiar tune. When Colin reached over to twine her fingers with his, she didn't resist. Instead she closed her eyes and told herself that it was all part of the fantasy, something she could hold on to just a little longer.

They wound up stashing their clothes on the beach and taking a dip in the surf. Zoe swam out a few strokes, enjoying the extra buoyancy of the salt water, then stopped to float on her back in the sun-dappled water. Colin came up out of the water next to her, water sluicing off his golden hair and skin. He pulled her close, nose to nose.

They didn't kiss, just stared into each other's eyes. His green gaze was languid, full of provocative promises. In response, Zoe felt a tug on her heart more dangerous than any undertow. "We'd better be heading back," she murmured.

He nodded and released her. They swam back to shore and gathered their things, then returned to the wharf, both of them preoccupied.

Dusk was falling as they shoved off. Colin lowered the outboard and they motored across, pulling into the slip just moments later. Zoe helped him to secure the boat, then they walked to the hotel, talking about the weather, the view and the activity around them. She felt prickly and nervous again, knowing that the time was drawing near for her to say what needed to be said. They walked through the hotel lobby and Colin punched the button to call the elevator.

"Do you want to get some dinner?" he asked.

She shook her head. "Thanks, but I'm really tired. I don't think I've completely adjusted to the time difference."

He nodded, but seemed antsy. "I'll walk you to your room." They rode the elevator to her floor, him looking up, her looking down. When they alighted, she walked two steps ahead of him, rummaging for her room key. When they reached her door, she turned.

"Colin, thank you for today."

He smiled and her resolve weakened. "You're welcome, Zoe. It was fun."

"Yes." She wet her lips. "I think it's always nice to end on a high note."

He looked confused for a few seconds, then his eyes widened. "Ah. You're giving me the heave-ho."

"I think it's best if we say goodbye now before there are any more complications for both of us."

He nodded. "I've been having the same thoughts. I guess I didn't consider the fallout."

"Good. Then we're in agreement."

"It would seem so."

Zoe stuck out her hand. "It was nice."

He glanced at her hand, then extended his and folded hers inside. His green eyes reflected amusement mingled with regret. "Yes, it was…nice."

Her fingers started to tingle, and not from lack

of circulation. Zoe withdrew her hand. "Okay. Goodbye then."

He took a step backward. "Goodbye, Zoe. Have a nice life."

"You, too," she murmured.

He maintained eye contact as he backed way, and then he was gone. Zoe wasn't prepared for the hollow feeling that ballooned in her chest. She opened her room door and walked inside, blinking back sudden, absurd tears. She must be more tired than she thought because she couldn't possibly miss this man, not after so short a time. Not when breaking off their arrangement was the right thing to do. So she could spend her last three days alone, thinking about the wedding.

She picked up the bag that held her "Zoe and Kevin's Wedding" binder, and the purple envelope containing the letter fell into her hand. The erotic, challenging words she'd written to herself came back to her in a rush.

Zoe pressed her lips together.

Three days alone. Thinking about the wedding.

She snatched her room key and headed toward the door. Had Colin had time to reach his room yet? If not, maybe she could still catch him.

But just as she put her hand on the knob, a knock sounded. She jumped, then checked the peephole.

A pair of bottle-green eyes looked back at her.

Her heart lifted, but she forced herself to take a calming breath. He could've come back for a lot of reasons. Maybe she'd left something in his room.

Or on his boat. Or maybe he was rescinding her free spa services.

Zoe schooled her face, then swung open the door. "Yes?"

Colin looked adorably hesitant, then jammed his hands on his hips. "I was wondering if you'd like to go with me to my ranch in Canberra for a few days."

Her eyes widened. "To your ranch?"

"It would give you a chance to see some of the outlying country. And…you'll have your opals."

Zoe frowned. "Opals?"

"There's an opal field on the ranch—not a big one, but it's produced some decent black opals…. You can have your pick."

Zoe's mouth watered. "Black opals?"

"The rarest, most beautiful opals that Australia has to offer."

She nodded, in awe. "I know."

A slow, cocky grin curved his mouth as he spanned the doorway. "And we'll have privacy. If you want to, we could pick up where we left off."

Inside her tennis shoes, her toes curled.

"What do you say?" Colin asked.

Zoe considered his offer and the ramifications. She wavered and waffled, shifting back and forth. Finally, she lifted her chin. "Only if you bring the handcuffs."

12

COLIN OFFERED HIS ARM TO HELP Zoe climb into his gray SUV, but she fairly bounced up into the seat. She'd forgotten how good it felt to be excited about visiting a new place, the way it had been when she'd first begun traveling.

"How soon until we get there?"

Colin laughed at her enthusiasm. "Pace yourself. It's a three-hour drive."

She reached up to pull out the seat belt, but he took it from her. "Allow me."

Zoe sat back, pleasure curling in her stomach as he drew the belt across her body and clicked it home. Then he gave the belt a yank to pull it more snugly over her lap. Zoe sucked in a sharp breath.

His eyes danced with amusement. "Tight enough?"

Zoe wet her lips. "It could be a tad...tighter."

He gave the strap another yank. "Now?"

"That's good," she murmured.

"Are you sure?" he asked, running a finger under the belt, grazing her mons through the khaki cargo shorts—one of the pieces of sturdy clothing delivered from a local shop, compliments of Colin. "Thought you might need these. C.", the note had simply read.

Perspiration beaded on her upper lip. How was this man able to turn an innocent activity into foreplay? "Yes."

He took his time withdrawing his hand. "Guess we're ready."

"Did you remember our...hardware?"

Colin picked up a small duffel bag at his feet and held it high, the contents giving a telltale clank. "Now can we go?"

She smiled and nodded. He closed her door, then walked around the back of the vehicle, lifted a window and deposited the duffel inside next to their luggage.

When he climbed into the driver's seat and closed the door, Zoe had to suppress a shiver of anticipation at the thought of spending the next two days with Colin. He was dressed in long cargo shorts, a loose button-up shirt and rugged hiking boots, all of them earth-toned and weathered. He looked strong and bursting with health, and so sexy that she itched to touch him.

Zoe fingered the collar of the shirt she wore that was made out of some hi-tech fabric to wick moisture away from the body. Her boots were new, too. She almost asked him how he knew her sizes, but considering he'd spent the past few days measuring her with his tongue...

"Thanks again for the clothes. You shouldn't have gone to the trouble."

"Nonsense," he said, turning the ignition. "I wouldn't expect you to have the right clothes for the station."

"Station?"

"Our word for *ranch*," he clarified, then pulled away from the hotel into light traffic headed out of Sydney.

"Tell me about your ranch," she said. "Is it big?"

He gave a little laugh. "It's not huge, but it's a good size. About two hundred hectares—five hundred acres. It butts up next to my brother Owen's station."

"You said your brothers were cattlemen. Do you have cattle, too?"

He nodded. "But not as many as Owen. I have sheep, too. And a few goats to graze the scrub."

"Does your other brother live nearby, as well?"

"Nah. Max has a big spread in South Australia. He's a serious cattleman. Owen and I just play at it." He grinned. "It gives us something in common with our dad."

"Your parents live close by?"

"Close enough to visit whenever they want, but not so close that my dad feels obligated to look after things when I'm not there."

"You have a station manager?"

"Right. And a handful of jackaroos."

Zoe frowned. "Are they dangerous?"

His laughter boomed out. "I think you'd call them cowboys. And generally, they're pretty safe."

She laughed sheepishly at her mistake. "Tell me what it's like there."

He shrugged. "The land is wild, but not as wild as the Outback. It's a working farm, so there's always something going on."

"Do you spend a lot of time at your ranch?"

He shifted in his seat. "Not as much time as I'd like."

She'd hit a nerve—perhaps Lauren Rook didn't care for country-living. "Do you have horses?"

"Sure. Do you ride?"

"My uncle used to have a stable north of Atlanta and I worked for him during the summer. But I haven't ridden in years."

"No worries," he said with a smile. "Your body never forgets."

Zoe's stomach tingled. She could attest that her body had a good memory where Colin was concerned. Every square inch of her could recall a different touch, lick or bite.

"Did you grow up on a ranch?" she asked.

"A small one, when I was very young. Then I got into soccer, and my family moved to a more populated area so I could compete at a higher level."

She chose her words carefully, loath to admit she'd looked him up online. "When I first met you, I wondered if you were a professional athlete."

"Ten years. With the knees and back to prove it."

"You seem pretty nimble to me," she said lightly.

He laughed. "You never saw me soaking in a hot bath after one of our games."

"I'd like to," she teased, then grew serious. "Do you miss soccer?"

"Not really. I enjoy the hotel industry much more than professional sports. I intend to make a name for myself in luxury properties."

A thought suddenly occurred to her. "Is that why you were in Atlanta on business? Are you looking at property in the metro area?"

"That's right. I've been working on a deal there for quite some time."

The news that he might someday have a reason to be in Atlanta on a regular basis—or maybe permanently—left her feeling out of sorts. "And what are the chances that the deal will go through?"

"I'm still very hopeful," he said, but she could tell he was distracted and didn't want to discuss it further.

Zoe was quiet with her own troubling thoughts. She'd assumed that when she left Sydney, she and Colin would never see each other again. She chided herself—this was precisely why they should've stuck to their original agreement not to ask personal questions. Too much information could be a bad thing.

She glanced at Colin's handsome profile, his forehead creased in thought. How would she feel if he was living only a few miles away?

It doesn't matter. You'll be married to Kevin and he'll be married to Lauren Rook.

"I forgot to mention," Colin said, nodding to her

bag, "that we won't have cell-phone service on the station, so if you need to make a call, you should do it before we get out of range."

"I suppose I should check my e-mail," she murmured, pulling out her phone and initiating the download. "My mother is driving me a little batty."

Sure enough, her phone beeped eight times, seven of them messages from her mother, and one from Erica, who was fond of putting her entire message in the subject line:

I miss the Aussie men. Hope U R misbehaving.

Zoe bit her lip. If her friend only knew.

Her mother's messages were about—what else?— the seating chart. Zoe felt her blood pressure rising.

"Wedding details?" he asked.

She hesitated, then nodded. "I feel strange talking about my wedding with you."

"Why?"

"Isn't it obvious?"

He shrugged. "We're just having sex, Zoe. One doesn't have anything to do with the other."

Technically, it was true...so why did his words sting?

"So," he said cheerfully, "how many bridesmaids?"

"Six," she said, confused by his line of questioning.

"And how many opals will you need for the brace-lets you're making?"

Of course—the opals. An unbelievable opportunity, but his generosity made her squirm. "One for each will be enough."

He grinned. "Ah, I think we can do better than that."

There was that tug on her heart again. Zoe returned his smile, then pretended to be absorbed in her mother's e-mails. Colin turned on the radio, and they eased into comfortable small talk.

After stopping for tolls leaving Sydney, they made good time, since it was interstate driving all the way to Canberra. Zoe watched the passing landscape change from lush greenery and thick copses of trees to grassy pastures to scrub foliage, dry eucalyptus forests and hilly terrain. True to the yellow kangaroo warning signs along the highways, they saw several groups of the animals hopping along in the distance. No matter how many times she saw them, she still thought they were bizarre, amazing creatures.

Canberra was the country's capital, she learned, situated between the two largest cities of Sydney and Melbourne.

"Downtown Canberra is a thriving city," he said, "but we're going to the bushland outside of town."

After they reached Canberra, she lost track of the roads he turned onto, but noticed they kept getting more narrow and more rugged. Finally he slowed to put the SUV into a lower gear and turned to climb a steep but well-maintained crushed-stone road, announcing, "Welcome to Benbullen Station."

"Benbullen?"

"An Aboriginal phrase for *a quiet, high place.*"

She smiled and turned her head to take in the palm trees, pine trees and giant ferns that lined the road. "It's so green. And there are so many trees. I thought it would be all pastureland."

"The pastures are farther out. To the right is a registered rainforest plantation. It'll be ready for harvest in, oh, about twenty years." He slowed and pointed. "Look closely up in that gum tree."

Zoe gasped. "A koala bear."

"They seem to like it up here."

"I can see why," she murmured, soaking up the landscape. She pointed to a field of staked, waist-high plants snaking up a hill in long, even rows. "Are those grapevines?"

"Yup. We have a small winery. Remember the cabernet that you liked earlier in the week?"

She nodded and opened her mouth to comment, but was distracted by the appearance of a two-story rock-and-timber house with a sage-colored roof and wrap-around covered porch. It was beautifully situated on a rise, nestled among the trees. The lines were simple and the proportions exquisite, blending in with the landscape versus jutting out of it or towering over it.

"It's...perfect," she murmured, then glanced over at him.

He had stopped the SUV and was watching her closely. "I'm glad you like it."

"What's not to like?"

"The remoteness, the lack of conveniences...and the swooping magpies can be annoying."

"Sounds charming to me."

Colin smiled. "Let's go see."

He drove up to the house and parked in a separate garage that was large enough to house three or four vehicles. Nearby was an in-ground pool, the blue-green water beckoning. Colin carried their luggage to the house, entering through a set of French doors from one of the wide porches.

Zoe walked inside and was struck by the handsome combination of rosewood floors, stone walls and a staircase with wrought-iron railings.

"Colin, it's lovely," she said, turning to take in all the details. The lower level was open, featuring one large kitchen, dining and living space, separated only by the staircase. The first floor was surrounded on all four sides by sliding or French doors, giving the impression that the furniture was simply sitting in the woodlands.

"I called ahead," he said. "So the kitchen should be stocked for a couple of days." He jerked his head toward the stairs and retrieved their bags. "Come on up. The view is nice from the veranda."

Zoe watched Colin climb the stairs and was suddenly besieged by panic. This was beginning to feel too good. Too…right.

"You coming?" he called.

"Right behind you," she said, then gave herself a mental shake and followed.

The upper level was even more impressive, with open ceiling trusses and more windows with spectacular views of rolling grasslands. A central seating area featured a bar and home theater, with doors on either side, presumably leading to bedrooms.

"That's a guest suite," he said, pointing before pushing open the door to the left. "And this is where I sleep."

Zoe glanced inside the room and at the sight of the enormous bed made of rough-hewn logs, was struck with a sense of déjà vu.

It's always nice to get back home and sleep in my own bed.

This was the bed she had pictured him in scant minutes after they'd met on the plane—massive, primitive, unique. Her body went moist at the thought of climbing into it with him tonight.

"What a wonderful room," she murmured, forcing herself to take note of the other pieces of furniture, the Aboriginal art pieces. The rosewood floors were continued upstairs, but some other kind of material covered the walls. She touched the uniquely textured surface.

"It's cork," he explained. "It's a renewable resource. I'm thinking of incorporating it throughout my hotels." He gave her a naughty wink. "Good soundproofing, too."

She blushed.

"Would you like a tour of the station?"

"Absolutely."

"I'll get the four-wheeler ready, if you want to freshen up. Take your time, come down when you're ready."

Zoe was glad for the chance to be alone, to collect her thoughts and absorb her surroundings. Intellectually, she had known, of course, that they lived in different worlds. Colin's resort alone was an impressive holding, and then there was the sailboat, which probably cost a small fortune just to moor at Sydney Cove. Now the ranch…and doubtless many other properties and possessions that she didn't even know about.

What incredible luck to have hooked up with this man to share a fantasy week—Colin Cannon was the total package. The kind of man to make a woman rethink her priorities…

Then her gaze fell on the small duffel that held their props. She walked over and unzipped the bag to reveal the handcuffs and lengths of narrow chain. It was a jarring reminder of what this week was all about. *We're just having sex, Zoe.*

Then, unbidden, something else Colin had said slid into her mind. It was the night they had entered into their arrangement.

"I want to experience something exciting," she had whispered. *"Before I walk down the aisle. I have fantasies…."*

And he had responded, "So do I."

Zoe hefted the chains in her hands, her mind racing. She glanced all around the bedroom, looking for a way to facilitate what she had in mind. Then she looked up at the exposed wooden ceiling trusses and a wicked smile lifted her mouth. It would work.

There was no better way to put their relationship

back on solid sexual ground in her mind than to turn things up a notch. Tonight Colin would get as good as he'd been giving.

13

COLIN PUT THE CHEESE AND BREAD he'd brought for their lunch in a compartment on the four-wheeler and pushed it out of the garage. Then he checked the fuel level and tires and when he was finished, he checked them again. He paced off nervous energy and began whistling under his breath—anything to keep his mind from going where it was going.

He wasn't developing feelings for Zoe Smythe— that would be just plain stupid. She had a fiancé waiting for her on the other side of the world, and meanwhile Lauren was tapping her foot waiting for a big, fat ring to seal *their* relationship.

He squeezed his eyes closed and conjured up an image of Lauren in his head. The woman was stunning, there could be no argument. They moved in the same social circles, had similar likes and dislikes, and her brother was not only one of Colin's best mates, but a valuable business partner. And as far as sex with Lauren…

He pulled a bandanna from his back pocket and wiped the perspiration from his forehead. Before

Zoe, he would've said that the sex with Lauren was good—great, even. But sex with Zoe…he'd never experienced anything so intense. Of the two women, Lauren was physically more beautiful, but she was plagued with self-doubt. Zoe, on the other hand, possessed an innate sensual quality that was so magnetic, she touched something inside him. She wasn't self-conscious, wasn't afraid to explore her sexuality, wasn't afraid to ask for what she wanted, wasn't afraid to moan—or scream—her pleasure. He couldn't get her off his mind. He'd had the perfect opportunity last night to walk away.

But he couldn't bear it. Couldn't bear knowing she was in the hotel, or even in the country, alone, when they could be together. Using the opals to entice her to Benbullen had been a flimsy excuse, but he'd been hoping that she, too, wasn't ready to let go of the fantasy they'd created.

At the sound of a door sliding closed, he looked up to see Zoe emerging from the house, her beautiful face lit with an enthusiastic smile. "I'm ready!"

But I'm not, he thought, his heart thumping in his chest. *I'm not ready for this. You're the wrong woman, it's the wrong time.* He managed to pull a smile from nowhere. "Let's go."

After climbing onto the four-wheeler, he helped her to settle on the seat behind him. There was a bar on the rear of the ATV she could've held on to, but he was happy to have her long, slender hands around his middle, caressing his stomach and holding on tight when they went over rough terrain and up hills. He showed her the most scenic parts of Benbullen, giving him the chance to see everything new through her eager eyes—the koalas, the wallabies, the cockatoos. He even noticed that the bloody swooping magpies—one of the winged devils had dive-bombed Lauren and taken a hank of her blond hair with it, traumatizing her to the point that she refused to leave the house when she visited the ranch—had a sweet, pleasing song.

They stopped at the winery to speak to his head winemaker and to sample the latest blends, and at the station manager's building for a general update. The temps were mild, but the dust left them thirsty. They stopped for their picnic lunch and to drink from a natural spring, then rode like children through the pear orchard where the trees were in full bloom and the blossoms snowed down on them. Zoe laughed in his ear and held on tight. Colin couldn't remember a more enjoyable day.

The sun was descending when they arrived back at the house, tired and hungry. He offered to let her shower first only because he knew they'd never make it to dinner and might perish of hunger if he joined her. So, exercising the extent of his cooking skills, he threw together a salad, selected a couple of bottles of wine from the cellar, set out a dish of dark chocolates and put on water to boil for linguini and shrimp. When Zoe came down looking dewy fresh and edible herself in snug denims and a light sweater, her dark, damp hair cascading over her shoulders, he stole a kiss and relinquished the kitchen to her.

As he climbed the stairs to the bedroom, the thought occurred to him that they were acting like an old married couple.

But that thought fled when he walked into the bedroom and saw two chains looped over a ceiling truss, hanging down, held together at the ends by the handcuffs. His cock jumped. This wasn't the kind of thing that old married couples did.

He was in and out of the shower in record time, then tossed on jeans and a shirt that he didn't bother to button. When he descended the stairs, she had found a music station on the stereo, had poured the wine and was straining the linguini. From the great smells emanating from the stove, she had found some garlic to add to the shrimp sautéing in a pan.

He came up behind her to help her with the heavy pot.

"Care to explain the contraption upstairs?" he murmured into her ear.

"It's for later," she murmured back.

He groaned. "Then let's get this meal over with."

Colin could barely keep his hands off her while they set the table—this fresh-faced, barefoot side of her was just as sexy as the made-up vixen. She sang along off-key to the American songs playing on the stereo and danced. Her mood was contagious. They talked and laughed over bowls of shrimp linguini and drank the buttery chardonnay from the station winery that he was most proud of.

"It's delicious," Zoe said, tilting her glass. "I'm so impressed."

He grinned wickedly. "Only with my wine?"

She angled her head. "Are you fishing for compliments?"

"Yes," he said, taking her hand and turning it palm up. "Tell me how good I make you feel." He plucked one of the dark chocolates from the dish and closed her hand over it.

She laughed and tried to pull away. "It's going to melt."

He held her fingers closed. "I know. You were saying how good I make you feel?"

She lifted her chin. "You're putting words in my mouth."

Colin opened her fingers, now covered with the dark, sticky chocolate. Holding her gaze, he lifted her hand to his mouth and began licking the chocolate from her fingers. Her lips parted and a sigh escaped her. Colin drew each finger into his mouth one at a time and sucked it clean.

She moaned.

"What was that?" he asked, angling his ear toward her.

A smile curved her mouth. "That feels...good."

Working in small circles, he licked the sticky sweetness from her palm. Her eyes became hooded and her shoulders loose. "You...make me feel good."

He laughed softly against her hand. "Let's go upstairs."

She nodded and he pulled her to her feet, already thinking about the way he was going to secure her with the handcuffs, the things he was going to do to make her feel so very good.

They were undressing each other before they got through the door. When they were both naked, Colin guided her to stand between the chains. He opened the handcuffs and gave a little laugh. "I'm not sure how these things work."

"Let me show you," she said, moving behind him.

He felt a tug on one wrist to his back, then the other, then two distinct clicks. And his eyes flew wide with the realization that *he* was the one being restrained. He pulled his hands apart and the handcuffs clanked. Zoe came to stand in front of him, a wicked smile on her face.

"You planned this," he said with a little laugh. Even as he said it, his cock was growing rock hard.

She nodded and held up the key to the handcuffs. "But you can stop me anytime. Remember our safe words?"

Colin nodded, still disbelieving that the little vixen had gotten the drop on him…and bloody glad that she had.

"So how do you feel?" she asked.

His throat convulsed. "Green."

She had to tiptoe to kiss him, rubbing her amazing breasts against his chest. He lowered his head to hungrily meet her mouth, but she had positioned herself well—to be almost out of reach of the chains. As she toyed with kissing him, leaving him unsatisfied, she encircled her hand around his erection and gave it a squeeze.

He gasped and thrust forward in her hand, leaving moisture on her bare belly. She lowered her mouth to his nipples and tongued them, still stroking the length of him. The sheer intensity of the sensations caught him by surprise—not having the use of his hands made him more aware of what was being done to him. He also had a new appreciation for the trust she'd shown in him for allowing him to restrain her. He was at her mercy, and he wasn't sure what to expect.

Which made his blood run even hotter.

She took the tip of his flat nipple between her teeth and bit down—hard.

He shuddered at the flash of pain and his cock surged.

"You okay?" she murmured.

"Yes…I mean…green."

She bit down harder, this time making him flinch. Then harder…and harder.

"Yellow," he said finally, exhaling loudly.

She eased up, laving the nipple gently before moving to the other nipple and biting down with increasing pressure until he sucked in a sharp breath and muttered. "Okay—yellow."

His cock was twitching in her hand. She brought

her body closer to his and used the head of it to stroke her clit. He groaned at the moist warmth of her and longed to push inside her. Instead she squeezed him harder and began to masturbate using him. Colin thought he was going to explode.

He ached to touch her. He rattled the handcuffs, but knew that ultimately, it would be more satisfying for both of them if he played out the game. She reached up and pulled his mouth down to hers, kissing and nipping him while she stroked herself using him, squeezing him harder and harder. His breath rasped out, and he nearly lost his balance.

"You okay?" she murmured.

"Green," he moaned.

She moaned her approval, then lowered her mouth to his collarbone and bit down as her body began to convulse. Colin was still, allowing her to pleasure herself, but he'd never felt so engorged. His balls twinged with an unspent orgasm. He gritted his teeth as he fought for control.

When her body quieted, she kissed him again, sighing into his mouth. Then she slid down his body to her knees. Colin groaned in anticipation.

Her tongue snaked out and stroked him from base to tip. He arched forward, but again, she was just barely within reach. She took the shiny head into her mouth and grazed her teeth over it. With her hand she squeezed his balls and stroked the sensitive ridge underneath. The torture was exquisite. He planted his legs wider to give her better access.

She alternately tongued and grazed her teeth over the length of him, then took him into her mouth as far as she could. Colin tightened his arms for leverage against the chains. The handcuffs were cutting into his wrists, pulling on the hair of his arms—the dull pain only made everything else more intense. Her tongue and teeth felt so good, stroking him, milking him. He set his jaw against the unbelievable pressure building inside him.

"I'm going to come," he groaned.

She pulled his erection out of her mouth and continued stroking him, sandwiching his cock between her ample breasts. The sight alone put him over the edge. He thrust forward, contracting his hips as the life fluid spilled out of him and over her breasts. The release was so intense, it bordered on pain. He grunted, then cried out her name, registering distantly that it was the first time he'd ever called a lover by name in the heat of passion.

Bloody hell, he thought fleetingly as his big body shuddered. That couldn't be good.

14

WHEN ZOE OPENED HER EYES the next morning, filtered sunlight streamed through the sliding-glass door. Colin was still asleep and from the sound of his deep, even breathing, he would be for some time.

Feminine satisfaction filled her chest—last night had worn him out. Her gaze moved to the chains still hanging from the ceiling truss, the handcuffs dangling at the ends. Her body tingled pleasantly with its own memories.

She quietly slipped from the bed and gathered clothes on her way to the bathroom, where she dressed and pulled her hair back into a ponytail. When she emerged a few minutes later, Colin hadn't moved, his big body still taking up a good portion of the big bed. He seemed to have no use for bed covers and was lying nude on his back. She took the opportunity to study his long, muscular body covered with light-colored hair. Even in sleep he looked powerful, his sex thick against his thigh. A shiver of appreciation ran through her. The man was a specimen.

She left the bedroom and pulled the door closed behind her, then padded downstairs. It was a beautiful morning, the trees and grass outside the glass doors brilliantly green and heavy with dew. She opened the French doors on the sunny side of the house to usher in the warmth and fresh air. The songs of birds and insects filled the room. Zoe sighed in contentment. Benbullen was a beautiful place.

She was drawn to the photographs sitting on a bookshelf. There were some of Colin in his soccer days, in uniform and in action. One of him with two other men who looked so much like him they had to be his brothers. And one with his brothers and a couple she presumed to be his parents. His father was as tall as Colin, thick-necked and balding. His mother was petite with dark hair, very pretty with engaging, bright eyes. And there was a picture of Colin with a woman she recognized as Lauren Rook. They looked like the golden couple, blond, fit and gorgeous. The frame was different from the others, more feminine. It was probably a gift from Lauren, Zoe guessed.

Not that it was any of her business.

The aftermath of their dinner littered the kitchen, dirty pots and pans in the sink, plates and glasses on the table. Zoe began clearing the mess and loading the dishwasher, making as little noise as possible so she wouldn't wake Colin, and started a pot of coffee.

At the sound of footsteps on the porch, she looked up, startled to see a man and woman standing there.

Zoe recognized them from the photographs as one of Colin's brothers, probably Owen since he lived nearby, and Colin's mother. Zoe froze, unsure what to do. They were talking and walked in through the open doors, not noticing her at first.

The woman was the first to see her and react. Her eyes went wide, then she stopped and put a hand on the man's arm, cutting him off midsentence. He looked up and stared.

"Hello," Zoe ventured nervously, wiping her hands on a kitchen towel.

"Hello," they chorused, although it sounded more like a question.

"I'm Zoe Smythe," she said over the awkwardness, supremely grateful to have taken the time to put on a bra.

"I beg your pardon," the woman said, recovering. "We didn't mean to barge in. We thought… That is, I'm Colin's mother, Virginia Cannon."

The man was still agape until his mother elbowed him. "And I'm Colin's brother Owen." He squinted. "You're American?"

"My brother Owen isn't the smartest of the Cannon boys," Colin said drily from the stairs.

Zoe looked up to see him walking down, fully dressed, thank goodness, but buttoning his shirt. He looked at Zoe. "As you can see, it's rather casual around here." He stopped and lowered a kiss on his mother's cheek, but he gave both her and his brother a bemused look. "How did you know I was here?"

Owen frowned back. "I heard the ATV yesterday and saw you driving around. Mum was staying with me and we thought we'd pop over to see how things went in Atlanta. We didn't realize you were trying to avoid us."

"Maybe we should come back another time," his mother said, turning toward the door.

Colin sighed. "No, Mom, stay."

"Don't mind if we do," Owen said, his voice and expression bursting with curiosity as he looked Zoe up and down.

Colin shot Zoe an apologetic glance.

"I made coffee," she offered cheerfully.

"And it smells wonderful," Virginia Cannon said, also clearly glad to stay. "Your accent sounds familiar. Are you from the southern United States?"

"Atlanta, born and raised," Zoe said. "Colin told me that you're also from Atlanta."

The woman dimpled. "That's right, in Virginia Highland."

Zoe smiled. "What a lovely area. I was raised in Candler Park."

"Equally lovely," Virginia said, then looked wistful. "Although I haven't been back in more than twenty years—I'm sure things have changed."

"Probably not as much as you think. There's just more traffic." Zoe leaned forward to look at the frog pin on the woman's shirt. "What a lovely pin. Is it lapis?"

Virginia fingered it and nodded. "I collect pins."

"Zoe makes jewelry," Colin offered, pouring coffee for all of them.

"Really?" Owen asked, still sizing her up.

"Only as a hobby," she said quickly.

"I offered her some of the Benbullen opals for a project she's working on," Colin said, handing a cup of coffee to Zoe. He gave her a meaningful look. "That's why we came up."

"Mighty generous of you," Owen offered when Colin extended him a cup. "Bro, what happened to your hands?"

Zoe glanced at Colin's hands, chagrined to see that the handcuffs had chafed red marks on his wrists. She nearly choked on her coffee.

"I sailed to Manly the day before yesterday," Colin said easily. "They must be rope burns."

"Indeed," Owen said, grinning into his cup.

Zoe's face flamed and she hoped the innuendo was going over Mrs. Cannon's head.

Colin glared at Owen and handed a brimming cup to Virginia. "We're riding to the opal field this morning, Mother. Would you like to come with us?"

"I wouldn't want to intrude," Virginia said, shaking her head.

"Nonsense," Colin said. "We haven't been fossicking in a long while. Your birthday is coming up. If you find a stone you like, we'll have it made into a pin."

His mother blushed. "That might be nice."

Owen rolled his eyes and looked at Zoe. "It's

hell being the son who doesn't have an opal field on his land."

Zoe laughed, enjoying the dynamic between them.

"So, Zoe, are you here visiting?" Owen asked, looking back and forth between her and Colin as if to see who would respond.

"Yes," she said. "In fact, I'll be returning to Atlanta tomorrow evening."

"We're heading back to Sydney in the morning," Colin offered.

"How did the two of you meet?" Owen pressed, sipping his coffee and looking innocent.

Zoe deferred to Colin, relatively sure he wasn't going to reveal that they'd met on a plane and had carnal knowledge of each other before disembarking.

"Zoe's staying at the resort," Colin said stiffly, giving his brother a stern look. "I'd invite you to go with us today, too, but I'm sure you have work to do."

"Not really," Owen said congenially. "I wouldn't miss this."

After they finished their coffee, Colin arranged for them all to meet at the stables. After his mother and brother left, he turned to her, hands on hips. "Sorry about that."

She smiled. "I don't mind. I just hope my being here isn't going to cause you any trouble."

He hesitated and she wondered if he would finally mention his girlfriend—it was obvious he was thinking of her. Instead he winked. "No worries. I thought we might head on over to the stables in case you want to practice a bit before Mother and Owen meet us there."

"Thanks, I'd like that."

He gestured around the kitchen. "It was nice of you to clean up, but I have someone to come in and do that sort of thing."

Zoe tingled with embarrassment, feeling like a peasant. "When I'm not in a hotel, I'm accustomed to cleaning up after myself."

From the look on his face, he realized his gaffe. "I just meant I wanted you to feel like a guest in my home, that's all."

She returned a smile. But she nursed a pang of sadness because she felt as if his offhand statement was the beginning of the end of the fantasy she'd spun in her head. They lived very different lives. And their time would be up soon.

Colin walked across the room and unlocked a cabinet, then removed a small wooden box and carried it to the table. When he lifted the lid, Zoe gasped. Dozens of small cut and polished black opals the size of peas winked back.

"Did you find all of these on Benbullen?"

He nodded. "None of them large, but all of good quality."

She selected one and held it up to the light. The fiery colors emitted prisms in all directions. "They're lovely," she breathed.

"Take your pick."

She looked at him, then returned the opal she'd been holding. "I thought we were going to look for rough opal today."

"We are. But even if we find anything, it'll need a lot of work. These stones are ready to set."

He was right—it would take her hours and hours to cut and polish even a small amount of rough opal. "It's a very generous offer, Colin, but I would feel odd taking your opals for bracelets for my bridesmaids. Will you let me buy them?"

"No. Consider it my wedding gift to you."

She blanched.

"It's okay, Zoe, really. What else am I going to do with them?"

"Sell them?"

"You know that none of these stones are extremely valuable—they're too small. Trust me. I'd get much more enjoyment out of knowing that you have them than I would selling them in bulk to a Sydney jeweler."

And it wasn't as if he needed the few dollars the stones would bring, she conceded.

He nodded to the case. "Please. Take what you need for the bracelets, and then you won't feel pressured to find something today. We can just have fun."

She wavered, then smiled. "Okay. One stone for each bracelet."

"I give nice wedding gifts," he said. "How about three for each bracelet?"

She laughed in spite of herself. "Two."

"Okay. Two for each bracelet."

She chose them two at a time so each bracelet would have matching stones and dropped them in a tiny drawstring pouch he gave her. "Thank you, Colin."

"You're welcome," he said, his eyes smiling as he returned the box to the cabinet. Then he rubbed his hands together. "Now, let's go prospecting. I just know there's a giant black opal up there waiting to be found."

She smiled. "Let it be today."

They rode the ATV to the stables. Colin chose a lovely brown mare for her and Zoe saddled her, then rode around the paddock for a few minutes, amazed at how quickly the basics came back to her. Colin watched from the other side of the fence, nodding with approval as she rode by.

A few minutes later, Mrs. Cannon and Owen arrived in a pickup truck. Colin saddled a horse for his mother and she bounded onto the animal like a girl. Zoe marveled over the camaraderie of the Cannons as they rode, talking back and forth. She felt like an interloper, but unabashedly eavesdropped on their good-natured banter, especially from mother to sons.

A pang of envy struck her—she and her parents didn't have that kind of relationship. All her life she had felt like the arbitrator, trying to negotiate peace between them. She could only hope that the truce they'd called for her wedding would hold for a while. If her mother had been a little overbearing when it came to the wedding details, Zoe figured the respite from her parents' bickering had made it worthwhile.

Realizing she'd fallen behind, Zoe make a clucking noise and squeezed her knees, urging the mare forward. As they fanned out, riding past sheep and cattle, she almost pinched herself—what a thrilling adventure. They rode for a couple of miles, then climbed a steep hill. At the top sat a small backhoe and an outbuilding next to a craggy hole in a rocky outcropping and a huge mound of dirt.

Colin dismounted and walked over to stand next to her horse. "Do you feel lucky?"

"Yes," Zoe said, although she wasn't referring to the probability of finding an opal. Her heart still pounded from the exertion of riding and looking at Colin only made matters worse. His blond hair was wind-blown, his cheeks ruddy. He was so strong and so...*male,* he spoke to everything feminine in her.

He reached up to help her dismount and her body ignited against his as she slid to the ground. His green eyes smoldered with desire, but they were both mindful of their watchful company. Virginia averted her gaze tactfully, but Owen stared outright.

Zoe stepped back and relinquished the reins of her horse to Colin and watched as the brothers walked the horses to a shady tree and tied them off. Zoe chatted with Virginia about things they had in common, but was aware that under the tree, the brothers were squaring off.

And she didn't have to guess at the topic of conversation.

"Bro, what the hell are you doing?"

Colin scowled at Owen. "What do you mean?"

"I mean, what happened to Lauren?"

"Last I heard, she was still in New Zealand."

"The last you heard? Did you break up?"

"No," Colin admitted.

"Then who's Zoe?"

"A...friend."

"Oh, so that babe slept in the guest room last night?"

Colin frowned. "That's none of your business, Owen."

"Are you in love with this girl?"

"What? Of course not. We only met a few days ago." Although it seemed like much longer, he thought. "And she's going back to America tomorrow."

"So when the Atlanta deal closes, you plan to keep a girlfriend on each continent?"

"No," Colin said through gritted teeth. Then he scrubbed his hand over his face. "Benjamin is having second thoughts about the Atlanta deal."

Owen frowned. "Why?"

"Let's just say he'd like to see a partnership between me and his sister before he signs the papers for a partnership between his company and mine."

"All the more reason to stay away from this woman."

"I won't be seeing her again," Colin said. "She's getting married."

Owen's eyes bulged. "You're risking your relationship with Lauren and maybe the Atlanta deal that you've been working on for months for a woman who's getting married?"

Colin frowned. "Well, when you put it that way."

"Take my advice, bro. Have fun tonight and tomorrow when this sheila leaves, forget you ever met her."

Owen walked off, leaving Colin to berate himself for being such an idiot. Maybe all those hits on the soccer field were finally catching up to him. Maybe he *had* lost his mind. He was risking everything on something fleeting. Lauren and his business were there for the long-term. And Zoe... Well, hadn't he just given her a wedding present, for God's sake?

Owen was right, Colin realized. Tonight he'd have fun with Zoe, and tomorrow, he'd do his best to forget he ever met her.

15

THE TENSION BETWEEN COLIN and his brother wasn't lost on Zoe, but when Colin walked up, he gave her a reassuring wink. "Ready to start fossicking?"

"I have no idea what I'm doing. I've never been on this end of the stones I've worked with."

He laughed. "Follow me. It's simple really. Owen's going to use the backhoe to pull out a chunk of dirt." He unlocked the door to the outbuilding, revealing picks, sledgehammers, handheld hammers, shovels and screen-lined trays. "Then we'll sift through the dirt to find rocks, or *nobbies,* as we call them. If there's no color on the outside of the small ones, they get tossed. But we'll break open the big rocks because they might contain an opal on the inside." He cocked an eyebrow. "Not too glamorous. You still want to give it a try?"

"Absolutely," she said, picking up a tray. "Is this where you found the other opals?"

He nodded. "I was riding the four-wheeler one day looking for stray sheep, and I came upon this spot when I stopped to take a rest. I looked down and there was a rock with an opal in it just lying on the ground."

"Have you thought about having this area excavated?"

"Nah. It'd be a complicated venture to get that kind of equipment on the top of this hill, and chances are, there isn't enough opal here to make it worthwhile. Opals develop in clay seams, and there's no clay here like in Lightning Ridge in northwest New South Wales where the best black opals are mined. I'm guessing that whatever opals are here washed down from the ridge over time. It's just fun to look for them." He passed her a pair of heavy gloves and clear plastic goggles.

Zoe donned the gear and stood back while Owen operated the backhoe and dug into the rocky earth. Her enthusiasm for the outing had dimmed because she knew that Owen disapproved of her being there with Colin. Mrs. Cannon probably did, too. Were they close to Lauren Rook?

She could tell that despite putting on a congenial face, Colin, too, was unsettled by whatever his brother had said. His body language was stiff and a frown line had settled onto his brow. Mrs. Cannon was friendly, though, as she and Zoe began the dirty job of sifting through the shovels of dirt that the men placed on the screened boxes. Zoe asked her about her childhood and, under a wide-brimmed hat, Mrs. Cannon relayed stories of floating down the Chattahoochee River on inner tubes with friends, and the annual lighting of a giant Christmas tree at Rich's department store.

"It's Macy's now," Zoe said, "but they still have the tree lighting every year at Thanksgiving at Lenox Square."

"And do you go with your family?" his mother asked quietly.

Was the woman inquiring into her marital status? Zoe wondered. Had she noticed the tan line on Zoe's ring finger?

"Yes, my parents and I usually attend together," she murmured. With Kevin, but she didn't think she should say so. Which only made her feel worse. "Australia is so different from the States, so different from the South, especially. Did you have trouble adjusting when you first moved here?"

"Oh, sure," Virginia said. "Back then telephones weren't even common, so I could only write letters home." Then she smiled, her eyes twinkling. "But I had my Daniel, and my boys, so I was very happy. What's the saying? Home is where the heart is."

Zoe smiled. "What's your husband like?"

"Look at Colin and you'll know," the woman said lightly. "Big and handsome and intelligent, the kind of man that makes a woman forget about her plans."

Zoe swallowed hard and chose not to respond, instead concentrating on the process of filtering rocks from the dirt and throwing them onto a pile at their feet.

They settled into a routine, the women sorting the larger rocks and the men breaking them open with sledgehammers. Colin seemed to be putting more muscle into the job than necessary. In fact, he and Owen both appeared to be working out their frustrations with each other with every fall of the hammer.

"Boys," Virginia admonished, "this is supposed to be recreation, not a competition. And look, I think I found something." She held up a rock the size of a golf ball.

They all gathered around to see. Colin used a bandanna to rub away the dirt, then held it up and smiled. "Good eye, Mom." From the rock winked a tiny green opal. "I'll break it open to see how big it is."

He placed the rock in the bandanna, then used a smaller utility hammer to break it open. When he unfolded the bandanna, he fished out the piece with the opal, then made a rueful noise. "It's small, but it's something." He handed the rock back to his mother with a wink. "But where there's one, there's another."

Sure enough, within the next hour, they discovered three more rocks containing small opals—Zoe herself found two of them. She was flushed and thrilled and knew in that moment that she'd fallen in love with Australia and all of its wonders. Then she glanced at Colin under her lashes and worried that her feelings encompassed this man, as well.

He looked up at that moment and his gaze caught hers, his eyes solemn with some unidentifiable emotion—regret that they'd entered into such a frivolous liaison? She turned away, afraid he would see what she was feeling. It was a good thing she was leaving the country tomorrow. If she stayed any longer, she might be tempted to think she was falling in love with Colin.

As the morning turned into afternoon, everyone began to tire and grow frustrated at the lack of further discoveries. Yet Zoe could see how prospecting could become addictive. Each time she was sure that the next muddy rock she picked up would hold a treasure.

"Owen, dear, I think I'm ready to go back," Virginia said, pushing to her feet.

"We can all go, Mother," Colin offered.

"No, you and Zoe stay. Owen and I have intruded on you long enough." She threw Owen a stern look, then smiled at Zoe and extended her hand. "In case I don't see you again, young lady, it was nice meeting you. Talking to you has made me homesick for Atlanta."

"It was nice meeting you, too," Zoe said, accepting the woman's hand.

Owen said goodbye, too, tipping his hat. Zoe gave him a friendly smile, understanding that his opposition to her presence probably had more to do with what she represented than with who she was. Colin kissed his mother's cheek, then traded defiant looks with his brother before they rode away.

"I'm envious of your family," Zoe murmured. "You all really care about each other."

He gave her a little smile. "Yeah, they're a bit on

the nosy side, but they do care." Then he heaved a sigh and stretched his arms overhead. "I'm getting a little tired myself. How about you?"

She drank from a bottle of water and nodded, admitting the sun and the insects were starting to get to her.

"One more boxful of dirt," Colin said, wiping his neck, "then we'll call it quits and go for a swim."

"Sounds good," she said. She was starting to feel as if their time together was expiring quickly, as if an hourglass had sprung a leak.

Colin put a few shovels of dirt in the tray, then she picked through it, scrutinizing the smaller rocks for colorful specks, handing off the larger rocks for Colin to split. She rubbed the dirt off a fist-size rock she held and studied the dark surface. Then she squinted—was that a flash of color? She rubbed at the spot, her heart beating faster when she saw it was the brilliant aqua of an opal.

"Colin, I think I found something." She handed it to him. "Probably another small one."

"Still," he said, then wrapped it and gave it a solid whack.

When he opened the cloth, he was silent for a few seconds and Zoe exhaled in quiet disappointment. Then he lifted his gaze and grinned. "Now that's what I'm talking about."

He extended his hand and Zoe gasped. The opal was the size of a quarter, with an unusual bloodred center, bordered with green and blue rings. The black

opals got their name from having a blackish back-
ground for the colors to contrast more brilliantly.

"This is a real find, Zoe."

She picked up the opal, still surrounded by rough,
craggy bits of rock, awestruck at its beauty. "I've never
seen this kind of coloring. It looks like a poached
egg."

"It kind of reminds me of the Flame Queen stone,
a famous Australian opal."

She reverently returned it to the cloth. "The stone is
amazing. Maybe you can do something special with it."

"I'm going to," he said, then picked it up and
folded it into her hand. "It's yours."

Zoe gaped and shook her head, holding out her
hand to give it back. "Colin, that's ridiculous. I
couldn't possibly take it."

"Of course you can," he said, covering her hand
with his. "As a souvenir of our time together."

"It's too much," she protested.

"I don't think so," he said quietly, thumbing a
loose strand of hair behind her ear. "Take it. Maybe
someday when you're an old woman with grandkids
around your knees, it'll remind you of the wild,
wicked week you spent with an Aussie before you
settled down."

Zoe felt overwhelmed by his gesture. She took a
deep breath and collected herself before she opened
her mouth, determined to sound as casual as he did
about it. "Thank you. It's remarkable." Then she
conjured up a teasing smile. "When I'm an old

woman with grandkids around my knees, I promise I will look at this stone and remember the week I spent with you."

"Good," he said, his eyes turning smoky. "Speaking of which, the week isn't over yet. What do you say we head back for that swim?"

She nodded, holding on tight to the opal, knowing that when the time came, it was going to be hard to say goodbye to this man.

They took a circuitous route back to the house, riding over hills dotted with sheep and grazing cattle. They spotted brilliantly colored Crimson Rosella birds and two more koala bears. The thought entered Zoe's head that she could live happily on Benbullen, but she knew she was only perpetuating the fantasy. It was easy to romanticize the situation because it would never happen. Spending two days being entertained on a ranch was not the same as living on one.

Just as spending a week with Colin on vacation in bed was not the same as living with him, both of them busy with their careers, dealing with family and the mundane details of life.

After making herself face reality, she was feeling somewhat better by the time they reached the house. She tucked the amazing opal into another drawstring pouch, still in awe of the treasure. They had a late lunch by the inground saltwater pool. She donned a bikini and joined him for a lazy swim. They drank beer and whiled away the afternoon touching and dozing and generally enjoying each other's company. On the surface, Zoe was breezy and flirty, but deep down, she was very much aware that their time together was growing shorter, almost as if a clock were ticking in her heart.

Dusk was setting when Colin grabbed her hand and brought her fingers to his mouth. "I was thinking about a shower. Care to join me?"

Her breasts reacted instantly, coming to a point. "I'd love to." As she followed him into the house and upstairs, she wondered if he would use the handcuffs on her tonight. She shivered in anticipation of their last night together.

In his bathroom he turned on the shower, then slowly removed her string bikini, one tie at a time. Instantly, she knew something was different—his touch was softer, more gentle. He took his time undressing her. She liked it, she realized, this luxurious exploration. She pushed down his swim trunks and he stepped out of them. They clasped hands and pressed their naked bodies together. He kissed her, a warm, long, lingering kiss as they melded into each other's curves and planes.

Colin broke the kiss and pulled her into the shower with him. They slowly soaped and massaged each other, kissing and licking and soothing reddened areas chafed from bindings or impatient teeth over the past few days.

Zoe felt herself loosening inside, as if she were being brought to a slow boil. By the time they rinsed under the cool water, her breasts were heavy and achy in his big hands, her sex pulsing with need. He turned off the water, wrapped her in a fluffy towel, carried her to his bed and stepped back to look at her.

The sun was setting, casting long shadows in the room. Zoe sank into the soft bedspread and stretched like a cat, unafraid to preen for him. He wet his lips, then turned away. She assumed he was looking for something to bind her hands or her feet and her pulse pounded in anticipation. Instead, he returned with a condom, which he rolled on quickly. Then he climbed onto the bed and covered her with his big body, his eyes intense. She opened her thighs to cradle him, reveling in the way their bodies fit together.

He gathered her in his arms and kissed her slowly, exploring her mouth with gentle thoroughness. Zoe moaned, loving this new, tender side of him. She ran her hands over the muscles in his back, reveling in his strength, marveling that he could have such a light touch. He slid one hand under her hips and rocked her up to meet him, easing his thick erection inside her slowly, one inch at a time, until she had accepted his full length. Wrapped in his arms and around his shaft, she felt as if they were one.

She sighed in contentment and pushed her hands into his hair.

They eased into a long, slow, unhurried rhythm that allowed them to enjoy each nuance of separation, then reunion. For long minutes he pumped in and out of her with measured strokes, awakening an orgasm in her core, caressing it to life and nurturing it to blossom.

But it was the eye contact that left her breathless. He caught her gaze and held it through every sensual thrust, studying her face as if he wanted to ensure she was enjoying every second of his careful lovemaking. A climax swirled in her belly like thick, warm liquid in a vessel, climbing higher and higher to the brim. As the pressure built, he encouraged her with his eyes, thrusting harder and deeper now.

"That's it," he murmured. "I want to hear you come, Zoe."

His erotic words sent her over the edge in a gush of molten ecstasy. She cried out his name and contracted around him, opening her legs wider to pull him deeper inside. The orgasm rolled on and on, seeming to draw from every part of her body. Zoe had never experienced anything so glorious and intense. She bucked beneath him, riding the wave. Then Colin stiffened, arching his body into hers and grunting his release.

"Zoe…mmm, Zoe," he whispered against her neck.

She smiled and pulled him closer, their bodies pulsing in tandem.

They lay together for a long time. When Colin pulled back, he cupped her face and looked into her eyes. But Zoe wanted to hide because she realized at that moment, without the props and the fantasy sex, that sometime during the week she'd fallen in love with him. It was crazy and wrong. And the only thing she could save at this point was her dignity. Colin would never know that this week had meant more to her than they'd planned.

"That was nice," she said, trying to sound breezy.

"Yes, it was," he murmured, then rolled to her side. Within a few minutes he was dozing, but Zoe lay awake wondering how she was going to forget about Colin. What a bind she'd gotten herself into.

Eventually, though, she slept, curled into him, taking solace in his warmth. And hoping that morning was far, far away.

The next thing she knew he was gently shaking her shoulder. Her eyes popped open and from the sunlight filtering in through the window, she realized that morning had come.

And that something was wrong.

"What is it?" she asked, pushing the hair out of her eyes.

"Zoe," he said, looking solemn. "You need to call home. Your fiancé has been in an accident."

16

SHEER PANIC PIERCED Zoe as Colin's words sank in. *Your fiancé has been in an accident.* She lurched up, disoriented. "What? What happened? How do you know?"

"When your mother couldn't reach you on your cell," he said gently, "she called the hotel. My manager phoned to inform me before contacting the police, not realizing, of course, that you were with me."

Her eyes filled with horrified tears. "Oh my God. Is Kevin all right?"

"I don't know," he said, punching numbers into the handset he held. "You can use this landline to get out. Just dial the area code and the number when you're ready." He set the handset on the table next to the bed.

Zoe swung her feet over the edge, pulling the sheet around her nakedness. Tears of remorse rolled down her cheeks. She was on the other side of the world in another man's bed and Kevin could be lying in a hospital, fighting for his life...or worse. A sob escaped her.

"Here you go," Colin said.

When she looked up, he was holding a robe for her. Feeling wretched, she stood and fumbled into it, trying to cover herself from his eyes. He glanced away. After she tied the belt, she picked up the phone and sat back down on the bed. With a shaking hand, she dialed her mother's number, trying to do the math in her fuzzy head to figure out the time difference. "What time is it?" she asked him.

"Six in the morning here, 4 p.m. yesterday in Atlanta."

She nodded. The phone was ringing. Her heart jumped erratically in her chest. Her mother answered on the fourth ring. "Hello?"

"Mom—it's me."

"Oh, Zoe, thank God. I've been trying to reach you."

"I know. How's Kevin?"

She died a thousand deaths during her mother's silence. Kevin's boyish smile popped into her head. *Please, God, he has to be okay.*

"He has a concussion, and his arm was broken in three places. He had to have surgery to have pins put in."

Zoe put the phone away from her mouth and choked out a sob of relief. She looked up at Colin and mouthed, "He's okay." Colin's chest rose in obvious relief, then he discreetly left the bedroom and closed the door behind him.

She put her mouth back to the receiver. "Mom, what happened?"

"A truck driver tried to pass a group of them riding in Tybee and clipped his bicycle. *Two days ago.*"

She grimaced, knowing how easily an encounter like that could've turned out so differently.

"Zoe, where have you been? Kevin's been asking for you. Why aren't you answering your cell phone? When the hotel couldn't find you in your room, I was on the verge of calling the police!"

Zoe closed her eyes. "I'm sorry, Mom. I got the opportunity to go to a ranch in Canberra and look for opals and…" She swallowed the rest of the big, fat lie. "I didn't realize there was no cell-phone coverage here."

"Kevin could've died, Zoe, and we couldn't get in touch with you. You should've let someone know where you were going."

Her eyes welled again, but she tried to stay calm. "Someone at the hotel knew," she said. "That's how they found me. Is Kevin home?"

"He'll be in the hospital for a couple more days. He's in a lot of pain."

Zoe's eyes welled again. "What hospital?" She wrote down the information on a pad that Colin had left. "I'll call him as soon as we hang up."

"Do that. He's ready to put out an APB on his bride."

Zoe closed her eyes. If he only knew. "I'm heading back to Sydney this morning, so I should be in cell-service range in a few hours."

"What time will you be in Atlanta?"

In a Bind

"We land around nine in the evening. I'll go straight to the hospital."

"Visiting hours will probably be over," her mother said sourly. "Your father and I have been going over every day."

"Thanks, Mom. I appreciate it and I'm sure Kevin does, too."

"We'll all just be glad when you're home where you belong," her mother chided. "We have a wedding to finish planning, you know. How's the reception seating chart coming along?"

"Um, fine," Zoe lied, rubbing at the pressure building behind her breastbone.

"We'll see," her mother said in a disbelieving tone. But it was light punishment for Zoe, and she was willing to swallow it.

"I have to go, Mom. I'll see you soon."

Zoe disconnected the call and hugged herself, feeling as if she'd just been yanked back from some horrible precipice. She stared at her bare ring finger and the enormity of her betrayal to Kevin washed over her. He was lying in a hospital, in pain, recovering from surgery, worried about *her* because no one could reach her.

Her eyes filled up again, but she blinked the tears back, sniffing mightily. She needed to talk to Kevin, as soon as possible, and try her best to behave as if nothing was wrong. She picked up the phone and left the bedroom. Colin was standing in the far corner of the entertainment room, looking out the window. He turned when he heard her.

Zoe could barely make eye contact with him. "I'm sorry, but I need to make another call, if you don't mind."

"As many as you need to."

"I've forgotten the country code to dial out."

He walked over and took the phone from her, punching in several numbers and handing it back.

"Thank you," she said, then walked back to the bedroom, a stone of dread in her stomach.

COLIN WATCHED ZOE WALK AWAY and felt utterly helpless. And just a little bit guilty. If he hadn't invited Zoe to come with him, she wouldn't have missed the call about her fiancé's accident and neither she nor her family would be so upset.

She'd left the door ajar and he could make out her voice. He heard her say, "Hi, sweetheart, how are you feeling? I've been out of cell-phone range or I would've arranged to come back sooner. I'm so sorry I'm not there...."

Colin descended the stairs to give her more privacy. Besides, it bothered him more than he cared to admit to hear her talk like that to another man. He rubbed his hand across his mouth and cursed—of all the bloody bad timing. Irrational anger toward the faceless bloke in Atlanta billowed in his chest for robbing Zoe of her last few hours of fantasy, and for robbing Colin of Zoe.

Then Colin put a hand to his forehead and laughed at himself. He was angry at Zoe's fiancé for having an accident and taking her away from him so soon? What did it say when one man was feeling possessive of another man's bride-to-be?

That he was going mad.

At the sound of footsteps on the stairs, he turned. Zoe stood there, still wearing the robe.

"I'd like to get headed back to Sydney as soon as possible," she said.

"Of course."

"I can't get on an earlier flight back, but I'd feel better if I was at least in cell-service range in case… just in case."

"I understand. We can leave as soon as you're ready."

She stood there looking at him, as if she wanted to say something more. He waited. But she simply turned and slowly climbed the stairs.

ZOE DIDN'T WANT TO TAKE the time to shower, but she had to wash the scent of Colin off her skin. The warm sluice of water, however, brought back memories of the previous night, when they had washed each other and then made slow love on his bed without the benefit of any props.

And it had been amazing.

She closed her eyes and squeezed out a few tears for her foolishness. She'd gotten herself into this situation and she was lucky it hadn't turned out worse.

She was going home with a slightly bruised heart, but at least Kevin was okay. If he hadn't been—

She turned off the shower and dried quickly, twisting her damp hair into a knot at the nape of her neck. After dressing in her own clothes, she tossed everything in her suitcase haphazardly. The chains and the handcuffs still hung from the ceiling trusses, mocking her. She pulled a stool over and climbed up to remove them, embarrassed now at her antics. She took them down and put them inside the duffel bag that Colin had brought. No doubt he would toss it when he returned to Sydney.

Golden girl Lauren Rook didn't seem like the type to indulge in dark fantasies.

Zoe did take the time to find her jewelry case and fish out an item that had fallen to a far corner—her engagement ring. She slipped it on her finger, ruing the day she'd taken it off.

After zipping her suitcase, she left the bedroom and carried her bag downstairs. Colin looked up and met her, reaching for her bag. When he took it from her, she noticed him glance at her engagement ring. Her face warmed, but he didn't say anything, just carried her bag to the bottom of the stairs.

"I'll just be five minutes," he said. "Then we can leave. I made coffee if you'd like some."

She poured herself a cup while she waited for him to pack. She felt numb and just wanted to get back to Sydney as soon as possible. To be away from Colin, to start getting him out of her head.

True to his word, he came back downstairs within a few minutes, carrying his suitcase. He turned off lights and shut things down as they were leaving, and then they were back in his SUV and leaving Benbullen.

Forever. The word came to her as they were riding past the gum tree where he'd pointed out the koala bear when they'd driven in. She laid her head back and settled in for the drive ahead.

"Zoe, I'm sorry," Colin said.

She looked out the window. "Don't apologize for something that isn't your fault."

"It isn't your fault, either."

She turned her head toward him. "What do you mean?"

"Your fiancé didn't have an accident because of what you were doing…with me."

His patronizing words sparked anger in her chest. "It doesn't matter, does it? He was hurt—he could've been killed—and I didn't know about it because I was with you."

His mouth tightened. "I'm just saying you shouldn't feel guilty about it."

"Well, I do feel guilty!" she shouted. "I *should* feel guilty! I'm going to be married in a few weeks and what I did to Kevin wasn't right. And what you did to your girlfriend wasn't right, either, Colin."

He frowned. "My girlfriend?"

"I know about her. I looked you up online. I saw her picture at the ranch house. And I saw the ring box

in your jacket on the plane. I didn't mean to snoop—
it fell out of your pocket when I went to get it for you."

He was quiet for a few seconds, then said, "I see."

"I convinced myself this was just a little fling for
both of us before we took the plunge, but I wasn't
prepared for how it would make me feel. And if you
don't feel guilty about what we did, Colin, then I feel
sorry for the woman you're going to marry."

His face darkened like a thundercloud, but he
didn't respond. Zoe didn't care—she needed the
anger between them. It helped her to distance herself
from him.

"Zoe—"

"Red," she cut in, falling back on their system of safe
words to get her point across. "This stops now, Colin."

She dozed until they reached Sydney. Her phone
woke her up because when they entered her service
cell, it went crazy beeping with unread messages.

Zoe, call me. Mom.

Zoe, you need to call me. Mom.

Zoe, your mom is looking for you. Call her. Erica.

Zoe, it's urgent. Call me now. Mom.

Zoe, Kevin's in the hospital. Where are you? Mom.

Zoe, it's Kev. I took a little spill and I'm okay, but
I'm worried about you.

Zoe, call me. Kev.

Zoe, I love you. Kev.

Zoe, where are you? Kev.

The pain and guilt washed over her anew. She glanced sideways at Colin, but he sat stoney-faced, looking straight ahead. When the hotel came into view, she was sure he was just as glad to get there as she was.

He pulled the SUV into the valet turnaround. Zoe unfastened her seat belt, remembering how excited she'd been when they'd left. An attendant opened her door and she climbed down. At the rear of the vehicle, Colin loaded her luggage onto a cart the bellman held.

"Follow Ms. Smythe to her room, please."

"Yes, sir."

Colin turned to her and gave her a flat smile. "I'm sorry things turned out the way they did, Zoe." He extended his hand to her. "Have a safe flight home, and…good luck with your wedding."

She'd needed things to end this way, but the dismissal in his face and body language hurt more than she thought it would. She swallowed the lump of emotion that clogged her throat and put her hand in his. A jolt of sexual energy lit up her arm, but she schooled her face into a passive mask. "Goodbye, Colin. Good luck with your wedding, too."

She withdrew her hand and turned to follow the

bellman, feeling Colin's heated gaze on her back as she entered the hotel. Did he hate her? Feel sorry for her? Or did he even give a damn?

She walked through the lobby, her mind racing, her resolve wavering. She could go back…thank him for sharing himself with her…for opening her eyes to a glorious world of sensation she'd never experienced…for introducing her to the ranch…for the lovely opal…

Zoe turned and saw through the revolving door that he had handed the keys to a valet and was walking in with a bellman, his own luggage on a cart. Her heart skipped in her chest, and she took a half step toward him.

But as soon as he crossed the threshold, a tall woman between them turned and spotted him, then shouted, "Colin!"

Long blond hair, impeccable clothing, body and face to die for—it had to be Lauren Rook. Zoe watched as the woman strode toward Colin, her arms outstretched. She saw Colin's look of surprise, then he mouthed, "Lauren," and accepted her embrace.

Zoe's heart squeezed painfully. And when Colin looked up and caught her gaze over Lauren's shoulder, she forced herself to turn and walk away.

17

Zoe drew the drapes in her room and slept until it was time for her to leave for the airport. She repacked her suitcase, now more crowded with the ranch clothes Colin had bought for her. She was tempted to leave them in the room, but it just seemed like such a waste to have them discarded. When she got back to Atlanta, she would take them to Goodwill.

She donned her flight attendant uniform, then shouldered her bag and left the room wheeling her suitcase behind her. As she rode the elevator down, she held her breath, eyeing the number for Colin's penthouse floor. Were he and Lauren in his room right now, having makeup sex? Had he given her the engagement ring, or was he waiting for a dramatic moment?

When the elevator doors opened to the lobby, Zoe exhaled and stepped out. She stopped at the desk to settle her bill and smiled at the clerk.

"Checking out, ma'am?"

"Yes, I arranged for a late checkout." She gave her room number and pulled her room key out of her purse.

The woman checked the computer screen and smiled. "You're all set."

"You can settle my account with the credit card I gave when I checked in," Zoe said, "but I need a receipt, please."

"There's no charge, ma'am."

Her eyebrows shot up. "Excuse me?"

The woman looked back to the screen. "Your room was paid by the house account, ma'am. I hope you enjoyed your stay."

"I did," Zoe murmured, biting her lip. Colin had either arranged for her room to be comped, or he'd paid for it himself. Either way, if she refused, she might have to face him again. "Will you please do me a favor?"

"Yes, ma'am."

Zoe reached into her purse and removed the drawstring bag that held the large red opal. She clasped it in her hand for a few seconds, then swallowed and handed it to the clerk. "Could you make sure this gets to Colin Cannon, please?"

"Mr. Cannon? Of course, ma'am."

She thanked the clerk, walked through the lobby and exited the hotel.

"May I get you a cab?" a bellman asked.

"No, thank you," Zoe said. "I have a stop to make first."

She walked the couple of blocks to Sydney Harbour, inhaling the salty air for the last time, she realized sadly. Fog was rolling into Sydney Cove, but the pier was crowded with bodies. She walked down to a corner railing and looked out over the blue, blue water. Then she reached into her purse and pulled out the purple envelope containing her letter.

The letter that had set all these reckless events into motion and turned her heart upside down.

She drew her arm back and winged the envelope as far out over the mist-covered water as she could. It skipped along the surface twice, then landed to float for a few seconds before sinking and disappearing into the depths of the bay.

"Good riddance," she whispered.

Then she backtracked down the pier and to the street to wave down a taxi.

"Where to, miss?"

"Airport," she said and swung inside. She took in the lights of the city as they were leaving, remembering the view from the rooftop garden—it was a beautiful place.

By the time she checked in at the departure gate, she was wearing her work face, determined to push all thoughts of Colin as far from her mind as possible. Between airport security and customs, she didn't have a lot of time to spare. They began prepping the plane and boarding first-class passengers soon after she arrived. To her chagrin, Jill and Jeremy Osbourne, the miserable married couple, boarded in her section.

She greeted them pleasantly, expecting to have her head bitten off, but the second honeymoon seemed to have worked because the couple was not only agreeable, but downright lovey-dovey as they settled into their seats, holding hands and making eyes at each other.

There were all kinds of marriages, she realized. She'd been wrong to think that just because she and Kevin weren't heating up the sheets, they couldn't be happy together. They would make it work. Kevin never had to know about her indiscretion with Colin. And she'd work very hard to make sure that she put it out of her mind, too.

In fact, once the plane lifted off, she closed her eyes and imagined flying away from Colin and flying toward Kevin. She invoked the imagery throughout the marathon flight as they progressed across the Pacific Ocean, landing in San Francisco to refuel and change crews, then flying on to Atlanta.

When she walked back to coach to find her assigned seat, she was happy to see Lillian, the woman with the jet-black, pink-streaked hair, sitting on the aisle. Zoe stopped to chat. "Did you enjoy your visit?"

Lillian smiled wide. "Very much. How was your trip?"

Zoe pursed her mouth. "Eventful."

"Did you get everything worked out for your wedding?"

"Not exactly.... But there's time to fix everything when I get back." She hoped.

"And the friend who wrote you the letter?"

Zoe shook her head. "I've decided not to see her. Some things are better left alone."

Lillian looked regretful. "If you say so. But I've always found that my closest friends are the people who knew me when I was young."

"Not this one. She didn't get me at all."

"Oh. Well, best of luck with your wedding."

Zoe thought of her reception seating chart, specifically, the spot at table five that needed a single person to sit between Mr. Dunbar and Mr. Wheaten. "Lillian, I know this is a bit last-minute, but would you like to come to my wedding?"

Lillian beamed. "I'd love to. I adore weddings."

Zoe tore off a scrap of paper. "Write down your address and I'll make sure you get an invitation."

Lillian printed her address, then handed it back. "I wouldn't miss it. Something tells me it's going to be interesting."

Zoe gave a little laugh and went to her seat. What an odd statement. But she waved it off and settled down to get some sleep so she'd be rested enough to visit Kevin at the hospital when she landed. She closed her eyes and tried to relax.

Away from Colin…toward Kevin…away from Colin…toward Kevin…

18

The following month

"ZOE, IT'S THE MOST LOVELY gift. I can't believe you made these," Erica said, her eyes misting. She and the other bridesmaids fastened their bracelets around their wrists, murmuring appreciation.

Zoe smiled at them all gathered around in her dressing room. "I'm glad you like them."

"Are these opals?" Erica asked.

Zoe nodded, feeling a bittersweet stab. "I got them when I was in Australia."

Erica leaned in to whisper, "At a ranch with no cell-phone service?"

Zoe bit down on the inside of her cheek. Erica had been dropping sly comments about "the Aussie in first class" ever since Zoe had returned from Sydney. Had she connected him to Zoe's vaguely explained inaccessibility for over two days? Zoe glanced away to collect herself. She didn't need this today. Not on her wedding day. Not when she'd worked so hard to get her mind to this place. Although the clothes Colin had bought her for the ranch still sat in a bag in the back of her closet, never quite having made it to Goodwill.

"Hey," Erica murmured, "I was only teasing."

"It's okay," Zoe said, trying to smile.

Erica frowned. "Are you all right?"

Zoe walked away from the group of women to a window, fanning herself. Outside, the church parking lot was filling with guests arriving dressed in their finest. All to witness her marriage to Colin—Kevin. *Kevin.* KEVIN. "It's just hot in here."

Erica trailed behind her, dressed in apricot head to toe. "But you don't look flushed. You look pale."

"Do I?"

"Zoe, are you having second thoughts?"

"No…of course not. I've known Kevin for six years. We've been engaged for three years. It would be pretty lousy of me to wait until the day of our wedding to decide he's not the guy for me."

Erica pursed her mouth. "No. It would be pretty lousy of you to marry the guy if you don't truly love him."

"But…I…do…love…Kevin."

Erica's eyebrows shot up. "You're going to have to be a lot more convincing at the altar. What's going on?"

Zoe hesitated, then pulled Erica close. "If you tell anyone what I'm about to tell you, I will kill you and bury you in that dress, got it?"

"Got it."

She pressed her lips together, then blurted, "I had an affair in Sydney with the Aussie from first class."

Erica's eyes widened. "I knew it!"

"But it gets worse."

"You're pregnant."

"What? No! I think I fell in love with him."

Erica exhaled loudly. "That is worse. How does he feel about you?"

"When I left, he was getting married, too."

Her friend made a face. "Bummer."

"Thanks a lot. The point is, I just don't know how I feel about Kevin. I know I love him, but I'm not sure it's the heart-pounding love I've always dreamed about. On the other hand, what I feel for Colin might just be infatuation because the sex was so…" She sighed. "Mind-blowing."

Erica elbowed her. "Do tell."

Zoe frowned. "This isn't exactly the place or time."

"Okay, later. Meanwhile, even if you do love this Colin guy, he might already be off the market, right?"

"Right."

"So the question is, can you forget a guy who's unavailable and who lives on the other side of the world enough to make a life with the guy who actually loved you enough to propose?"

Zoe pursed her mouth. "Good point."

"On the other hand, Zoe, I have to tell you that the day I married Jim was one of the happiest days of my life. And no matter how much I complain about him, I'd do it all over again in a second. Maybe you won't know until you look down the aisle."

Over the loudspeaker, piano music began to play.

Erica jerked her head toward the door. "That's our cue. What do you want to do?"

Zoe gave her friend's hand a squeeze. "Go. I'm being a basket case. Thanks for the pep talk."

Zoe watched her bridesmaids file out, a veritable apricot smorgasbord. Her mother came in, beaming. Today's festivities would truly be a nod to her, Zoe conceded.

"They're getting ready to seat us, dear. I just wanted to come back and tell you how proud your father and I are that you're marrying someone as nice as Kevin. He's going to be a good husband to you."

But will I be a good wife to him? "Thanks, Mom."

"You look absolutely beautiful. The dress, the veil—it couldn't be more perfect."

"Thanks to you," Zoe murmured.

"Yes, well, anything to give you a perfect start." Her mother sighed. "Sometimes I think the reason your father and I have had such a rocky time of it is because we didn't do things right, didn't have a nice wedding like this."

"Oh, Mom, that's not the reason."

Her mother smiled. "Well, that's not going to happen to you, because your wedding day is going to be perfect."

Zoe nodded. "Yes, it will."

A chime sounded and her mother jumped. "Oh, that means they're ready for me. I'll see you out there, dear."

She watched her mother scurry out in her beaded mother-of-the-bride dress. She had gone to so much trouble to give her daughter a fairy-tale wedding....

Zoe gave herself a mental shake. Colin probably hadn't given her another thought after she'd left Sydney. He was engaged to a stunning woman of his own class. He was far, far away. And Kevin was here, waiting to marry her.

The wedding director appeared in the doorway. "Zoe, it's time."

She took a deep breath, pulled her veil over her face and picked up her bouquet. She hadn't done the right thing in Sydney, but she could do the right thing now.

She met her father in the hallway and he gave her an encouraging smile. "You look beautiful, sweetheart, just beautiful."

"Thank you, Daddy."

They walked to the rear of the church and the bridal march began to play. Two tuxedoed ushers opened the double doors. Everyone in the packed sanctuary stood and turned toward her, beaming.

Except for one person, Zoe noticed. Her new friend Lillian sat in the back row and while she wasn't frowning, she wasn't smiling, either. Zoe's heart was thumping against her chest, her thoughts scattered and running wild. She thought of the letter that she'd written, the challenge to herself to find that one-of-a-kind love. Had she let herself down?

She looked down the aisle to her groom. Kevin was grinning back at her, surrounded by his tuxedoed friends, her bridesmaids and the minister, plus a cluster of flower girls and a ring bearer.

All. Waiting. For. Her.

"Are you okay, sweetheart?" her father whispered out of the corner of his mouth. And Zoe realized her feet weren't moving.

Zoe glanced to Lillian, who seemed to be telegraphing something to her with those incredible violet-colored eyes. Then she looked back to Kevin, whose smile had dimmed a fraction. She had to do the right thing.

She couldn't marry him.

Zoe handed her bouquet to her father. "Stay here, Daddy."

He gave her a concerned look. "Your mother will kill me."

She lifted her skirt with both hands. "You probably don't want to be next to her when I do this."

He blanched. "I'll stay here."

It took less time to dismantle the wedding than Zoe had imagined. Telling Kevin she couldn't marry him was the hardest part, of course. He kept looking at the ring she gave back as if it were going to explode. He was so incredulous, she truly felt sorry for him.

Seeing the look on her mother's face as the

ceremony went down in flames was the next hardest part.

"Zoe, have you lost your mind?"

"Maybe," Zoe confessed, then borrowed the minister's mike and invited anyone who still wanted to come to the reception dinner in the hall across the parking lot to please come, but added they were on their own as far as the seating was concerned.

"That," Erica said as everyone filed out of the church with baffled looks on their faces, "is the most courageous thing I've ever seen. I only have one question."

"What's that?" Zoe said miserably.

"Do we get to keep the bracelets?"

Zoe laughed and nodded, then gave her friend a hug. "Let's go eat chicken Kiev and wedding cake."

But Erica was looking past her shoulder. "Um, Zoe. Don't look now, but the Aussie from first class is standing in the back of the church."

19

ZOE'S HEAD JERKED UP. "What did you say?"

Erica pointed. "Aussie, back of church. I can't make this stuff up."

Zoe turned around and her heart vaulted to her throat. Colin was standing there dressed in a beautiful dark suit, staring at her. Her knees turned to rubber. She told herself to calm down. There could be lots of reasons for him to be in Atlanta. At this church. On her wedding day.

The church was almost empty now, except for a few strays—her mother, who was sitting in a pew, softly crying. Erica, of course. The minister, who seemed confounded to have lost his captive audience. And Lillian, in the back, who was watching Zoe and Colin closely. Zoe distantly remembered the woman's comment on the plane about attending the wedding.

I wouldn't miss it. Something tells me it's going to be interesting.

How odd. It was as if she'd known…. No, that was impossible.

Zoe walked down the aisle on unsteady legs toward Colin and stopped a few feet away from him. "Hi."

"Hello," he said and glanced around the empty church. "Did I miss the ceremony?"

"No. There was no ceremony."

He took a step closer. "That's…interesting."

She crossed her arms and lifted her chin. "How did *your* wedding go?"

"It didn't. I never planned to marry Lauren."

"But the ring box—"

"Held a pin I bought my mother for her birthday while I was in Atlanta."

She took a step closer. "You don't say?"

"I should've said so sooner, but I thought it was better to let you think what you wanted, to let you go."

"So what are you doing here?"

His Adam's apple bobbed. "I was trying to think of a good excuse all the way here."

She took a step closer. "And what's the best one you came up with?"

He took a step toward her. "That I love you."

She took a step toward him. "You waited until my wedding day to tell me you love me?"

He stepped forward and wrapped his arms around her. "We're going to have to work on our timing."

She looped her arms around his neck. "Okay."

He kissed her long and hard, reawakening the nerve endings in her body that had slumbered ever since she left Sydney. He lifted his head. "Marry *me*."

"Okay," she murmured.

He blinked. "That's it? You don't want to see the ring first?"

She smiled. "You have a ring?"

From his jacket pocket he removed a gray ring box and opened it.

Zoe gasped. The red-centered opal was mounted in a platinum setting, surrounded by a circle of diamonds. "It's…incredible."

He caressed her cheek with his thumb. "You once promised me that one day when you're an old woman with grandkids around your knees, that you would look at this stone and remember the wild week you had with me before you settled down."

"And I will," she whispered. "Except they'll be our grandkids."

Colin removed the ring and slid it onto her finger. "So you'll still have me?"

"Yes," she said, laughing.

"Don't you mean *green?*" he murmured, nuzzling her ear.

She moaned, already looking forward to their wedding night. "Let's get married now."

He pulled back and laughed. "Now?"

"Why not? We have a dress and a minister and chicken Kiev. I'll get Mother to scrape Kevin's name off the wedding cake." Zoe nodded to where her mother sat in the pew, her shoulders still shaking with sobs. "She'll be ecstatic that I'm marrying someone today."

"With an offer like that," he said drily, "how can I refuse?"

"Humor me," Zoe said, picking up the end of his tie. "I can't wait another day to be legally bound to you."

Colin grinned. "Well, when you put it that way…"

Epilogue

"CAN I GIVE THE ARTIST a ride to lunch?"

Zoe lifted her head from the opal necklace she was working on and smiled. "Only if you take it easy on the hills."

"I promise."

She moved awkwardly from behind the table, bringing herself and her big pregnant belly with her.

"You are beautiful, Mrs. Cannon," he said, kissing her thoroughly.

Zoe smiled up at her gorgeous husband and thought her heart might burst open. "You're lying, but this is what you get for getting me pregnant on our wedding night."

He grinned. "What can I say? My sperm finds your eggs irresistible."

"Speaking of eggs, I'm starving."

"Let's get you to the house."

She followed him out, then turned and locked the door to the Benbullen Artisan Jewelry Studio. She loved this place he'd built for her, loved what she was doing, loved Colin, loved their unborn child.

She removed an envelope from her bag and ran her finger over the address—Dr. Michelle Alexander, Covington Women's College. If she hadn't received her letter when she did, she might not have had the nerve to meet Colin in the lavatory on the plane. The letter had set all those magical, life-changing events into motion.

"Can we drop this at the post?"

"Sure. What is it?"

"A thank-you letter I've been meaning to send. Maybe I'll explain it one day."

"Okay. Ready, love?"

A one-of-a-kind love. Zoe smiled and nodded, linking her arm with his.

* * * * *

Don't miss NO PEEKING...the next blazing-hot book in the SEX FOR BEGINNERS trilogy by Stephanie Bond, available next month!

Here is a sneak preview of
A STONE CREEK CHRISTMAS,
the latest in Linda Lael Miller's acclaimed
MCKETTRICK *series.*

A lonely horse brought vet Olivia O'Ballivan
to Tanner Quinn's farm, but it's the rancher's
love that might cause her to stay.

A STONE CREEK CHRISTMAS
Available December 2008
from Silhouette Special Edition

Tanner heard the rig roll in around sunset. Smiling, he wandered to the window. Watched as Olivia O'Ballivan climbed out of her Suburban, flung one defiant glance toward the house and started for the barn, the golden retriever trotting along behind her.

Taking his coat and hat down from the peg next to the back door, he put them on and went outside. He was used to being alone, even liked it, but keeping company with Doc O'Ballivan, bristly though she sometimes was, would provide a welcome diversion.

He gave her time to reach the horse Butterpie's stall, then walked into the barn.

The golden retriever came to greet him, all wagging tail and melting brown eyes, and he bent to stroke her soft, sturdy back. "Hey, there, dog," he said.

Sure enough, Olivia was in the stall, brushing Butterpie down and talking to her in a soft, soothing voice that touched something private inside Tanner and made him want to turn on one heel and beat it back to the house.

He'd be damned if he'd do it, though.

This was *his* ranch, *his* barn. Well-intentioned as she was, *Olivia* was the trespasser here, not him.

"She's still very upset," Olivia told him, without turning to look at him or slowing down with the brush.

Shiloh, always an easy horse to get along with, stood contentedly in his own stall, munching away on the feed Tanner had given him earlier. Butterpie, he noted, hadn't touched her supper as far as he could tell.

"Do you know anything at all about horses, Mr. Quinn?" Olivia asked.

He leaned against the stall door, the way he had the day before, and grinned. He'd practically been raised on horseback; he and Tessa had grown up on their grandmother's farm in the Texas hill country, after their folks divorced and went their separate ways, both of them too busy to bother with a couple of kids. "A few things," he said. "And I mean to call you Olivia, so you might as well return the favor and address me by my first name."

He watched as she took that in, dealt with it, decided on an approach. He'd have to wait and see what that turned out to be, but he didn't mind. It was a pleasure just watching Olivia O'Ballivan grooming a horse.

"All right, *Tanner*," she said. "This barn is a disgrace. When are you going to have the roof fixed? If it snows again, the hay will get wet and probably mold...."

He chuckled, shifted a little. He'd have a crew out there the following Monday morning to replace the roof and shore up the walls—he'd made the arrangements over a week before—but he felt no particular compunction to explain that. He was enjoying her ire too much; it made her color rise and her hair fly when she turned her head, and the faster breathing made her perfect breasts go up and down in an enticing rhythm. "What makes you so sure I'm a greenhorn?" he asked mildly, still leaning on the gate.

At last she looked straight at him, but she didn't move from Butterpie's side. "Your hat, your boots—that fancy red truck you drive. I'll bet it's customized."

Tanner grinned. Adjusted his hat. "Are you telling me real cowboys don't drive red trucks?"

"There are lots of trucks around here," she said. "Some of them are red, and some of them are new. And *all* of them are splattered with mud or manure or both."

"Maybe I ought to put in a car wash, then," he

teased. "Sounds like there's a market for one. Might be a good investment."

She softened, though not significantly, and spared him a cautious half smile, full of questions she probably wouldn't ask. "There's a good car wash in Indian Rock," she informed him. "People go there. It's only forty miles."

"Oh," he said with just a hint of mockery. "*Only* forty miles. Well, then. Guess I'd better dirty up my truck if I want to be taken seriously in these here parts. Scuff up my boots a bit, too, and maybe stomp on my hat a couple of times."

Her cheeks went a fetching shade of pink. "You are twisting what I said," she told him, brushing Butterpie again, her touch gentle but sure. "I meant…"

Tanner envied that little horse. Wished he had a furry hide, so he'd need brushing, too.

"You *meant* that I'm not a real cowboy," he said. "And you could be right. I've spent a lot of time on construction sites over the last few years, or in meetings where a hat and boots wouldn't be appropriate. Instead of digging out my old gear, once I decided to take this job, I just bought new."

"I bet you don't even *have* any old gear," she challenged, but she was smiling, albeit cautiously, as though she might withdraw into a disapproving frown at any second.

He took off his hat, extended it to her. "Here," he teased. "Rub that around in the muck until it suits you."

She laughed, and the sound—well, it caused a powerful and wholly unexpected shift inside him. Scared the hell out of him and, paradoxically, made him yearn to hear it again.

* * * * *

Discover how this rugged rancher's wanderlust is tamed in time for a merry Christmas, in A STONE CREEK CHRISTMAS. In stores December 2008.

SILHOUETTE

SPECIAL EDITION™

Kate's Boys

MISTLETOE AND MIRACLES

by *USA TODAY* bestselling author

MARIE FERRARELLA

Child psychologist Trent Marlowe couldn't believe his eyes when Laurel Greer, the woman he'd loved and lost, came to him for help. Now a widow, with a troubled boy who wouldn't speak, Laurel needed a miracle from Trent...and a brief detour under the mistletoe wouldn't hurt, either.

Available in December wherever books are sold.

EXTRA

THE ITALIAN'S BRIDE
Commanded—to be his wife!

Used to the finest food, clothes and women, these immensely powerful, incredibly good-looking and undeniably charismatic men have only one last need: a wife!

They've chosen their bride-to-be and they'll have her—willing or not!

Enjoy all our fantastic stories in December:

REQUEST YOUR FREE BOOKS!

2 FREE NOVELS PLUS 2 FREE GIFTS!

HARLEQUIN®

Blaze™

Red-hot reads!

HB08R

HARLEQUIN® Romance®

Marry-Me Christmas

by *USA TODAY* bestselling author

SHIRLEY JUMP

A *Bride* FOR ALL *Seasons*

Ruthless and successful journalist Flynn never mixes business with pleasure. But when he's sent to write a scathing review of Samantha's bakery, her beauty and innocence catches him off guard. Has this small-town girl unlocked the city slicker's heart?

Available December 2008.

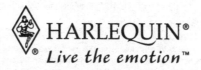

HARLEQUIN®
Live the emotion™

HARLEQUIN®

Blaze™

COMING NEXT MONTH

#435 HEATING UP THE HOLIDAYS
Jill Shalvis, Jacquie D'Alessandro, Jamie Sobrato
A Hunky Holiday Collection
Santa's finally figured out what women want—hot guys! And these three lucky
ladies unwrap three of the hottest men around. Don't miss this Christmas
anthology, guaranteed to live up to its title!

#436 YULE BE MINE **Jennifer LaBrecque**
Forbidden Fantasies
Journalist Giselle Randolph is looking forward to her upcoming assignment
in Sedona…until she learns that her photographer is Sam McKendrick—the
man she's lusted after for most of her life, the man she used to call her
brother….

#437 COME TOY WITH ME **Cara Summers**
Navy captain Dino Angelis might share a bit of his family's "sight," but even
he never dreamed he'd be spending the holidays playing protector to sexy
toy-store owner Cat McGuire. Or that he'd be fighting his desire to play with
her himself…

#438 WHO NEEDS MISTLETOE? **Kate Hoffmann**
24 Hours: Lost, Bk. 1
Sophie Madigan hadn't intended to spend Christmas Eve flying rich boy
Trey Shelton III around the South Pacific…or to make a crash landing. Still,
now that she's got seriously sexy Trey all to herself for twenty-four hours, why
not make it a Christmas to remember?

#439 RESTLESS **Tori Carrington**
Indecent Proposals, Bk. 2
Lawyer Lizzie Gilbred has always been a little too proper…until she meets hot
guitarist Patrick Gauge. But even mind-blowing sex may not be enough for
Lizzie to permanently let down her guard—or for Gauge to stick around….

#440 NO PEEKING… **Stephanie Bond**
Sex for Beginners, Bk. 3
An old letter reminds Violet Summerlin that she'd dreamed about sex that was
exciting, all-consuming, *dangerous!* And dreams were all they were…until her
letter finds its way to sexy Dominick Burns…

www.eHarlequin.com